REBELLIOUS HEARTS

Journalist Alice Jordan can't believe her misfortune when she literally bumps into entrepreneur Dominic Falconer. She is running a newspaper campaign to prevent him from destroying an ancient wood in his apparently never-ending pursuit of profit. However, when it becomes clear that local opinion is firmly on his side, Alice decides to go it alone. Someone has to stop him and she is more than ready for the battle. The trouble is — so is Dominic.

SUSAN UDY

REBELLIOUS HEARTS

Complete and Unabridged

LINFORD
Leicester

First published in Great Britain in 2010

First Linford Edition
published 2013

A catalogue record for this book is available
from the British Library.

ISBN 978–1–4448–1650–1

Published by
F. A. Thorpe (Publishing)
Anstey, Leicestershire

Set by Words & Graphics Ltd.
Anstey, Leicestershire
Printed and bound in Great Britain by
T. J. International Ltd., Padstow, Cornwall

This book is printed on acid-free paper

1

Alice Jordan's first reaction when she saw what she'd done was to clamp both hands over her eyes and pray to disappear — now, this minute.

She didn't, of course. So, instead, she gingerly parted her fingers and peered through the narrow gap, only to be met with a sight terrifying enough to make her snap them shut again.

A man, presumably the driver of the gleaming red Ferrari she'd just driven into the back of, was moving purposefully towards her, his expression formidable. In fact, he could easily have been mistaken for some sort of buccaneer, with skin that was so deeply tanned it was almost swarthy, and a nose that curved like an eagle's beak. Beneath this, she'd glimpsed a mouth that was twisted into a ferocious grimace. All he needed to complete the picture of menacing intent was a black eyepatch.

Bracing herself for what she suspected would be a fairly heated dialogue, she dropped her hands and met that stabbing stare head on — at the precise second that he came to a halt alongside her modest Ford Fiesta. He literally towered over her, six feet two — maybe three — inches of outraged manhood.

With fingers that trembled, she wound down her window. She caught a whiff of some very expensive aftershave. But then, a man who drove a Ferrari would hardly wear something cheap. She smiled grimly at the notion.

'Oh, you think it's funny, do you?' Eyes the colour of steel clashed with her green ones as his mouth tightened into an uncompromising slit.

Alice flinched away from him. 'N-no,' she stuttered, practically cowering behind the steering wheel by this time, positive that that searing gaze was about to strip the flesh from her. Although what protection she thought a steering wheel could offer, she couldn't have said.

He leaned down as if he were about to haul her out of the car.

'If-if you t-touch me, I'll — I'll — '
She'd retreated so far away from him that she only needed to move another inch and she'd literally be sitting on the passenger seat. She was already half on it.

'You'll do what, exactly?'

She thought she detected amusement in his eyes, then, but surely, that was impossible. Fury? Intent to murder? Yes. Amusement? Definitely not. Not after the way she'd damaged his precious car.

'I — I'll scream,' she whispered.

He snorted. Alice couldn't believe it. The wretched man was actually laughing at her. She scuttled back off the passenger seat and sat upright.

'Scream away,' he drawled, his gaze scanning the completely deserted road on either side of them. 'Although what good it will do you, I don't know.' His voice was as smooth as hot chocolate, all trace of fury gone.

If Alice hadn't seen the transformation for herself, she would never have believed it. One second he'd appeared ready to murder her, the next he'd been laughing. The man was inhuman. But inhuman or not, his next action was eminently sensible. He reached in and turned Alice's ignition off — something she herself should have thought to do. Feeling more than a little foolish, she glared at him. 'What do you think you're doing?'

'No,' he contradicted calmly, 'that's what I should be asking you. So what happened? Did you doze off? Not spot the other car coming? Get bored? What? It must have been more than obvious that I'd have to stop. It is a roundabout, after all. Small, I grant you, but still plainly visible — '

Bristling with indignation at his insinuation that she was either blind or downright stupid, Alice flung her car door open, causing him to take a hasty

4

step backwards to avoid it hitting him in the stomach, and climbed out. Miraculously, her fear had vanished. His sarcastic words had done that. 'No, I didn't see your car, I was looking the other way — '

'The other way! Do you make a habit of looking the other way to the one you're going in? That must make for a very interesting ride. Not one that I'd particularly care to share, mind you.'

Good grief. Did he have to make such a song and dance about it? It was only a car, after all, and she couldn't have done that much damage, she'd been hardly moving. Now, if he'd been lying on the road in front of her, he'd have had good reason to complain.

'Is there much damage?' She rearranged her expression into one of polite interest. She ought to make some effort to find out, she supposed.

But clearly he wasn't deceived. 'Why don't you look for yourself?' he ground out as he took hold of her arm, not quite dragging her the couple of yards towards the rear of his car, but pulling her forcefully enough to have her executing a series of neat hops and skips as she struggled to match his stride. The fact that she shed a shoe in the process only added to the indignity of the situation.

'Stop! How dare — ?' she gasped, too out of breath to say much more.

Mercifully, he did stop and Alice managed to yank her arm out of his grasp, before bending to retrieve her shoe. She didn't dare look at him, because if he was laughing at her again, she'd — well, she didn't allow herself to think of what she might do, only that it would make any damage to his car pale into insignificance. She slipped her foot back into her shoe and rejoined him, taking care to keep her arm well out of his reach.

She looked down to where the front of her car was touching his. 'Oh!' The two vehicles seemed to be welded together, and she could see a definite dent in the Ferrari's previously immaculate bodywork.

'Yes. Quite, Ms — ?'

'Jordan; Alice Jordan,' she said without looking at him.

'Ah. Alice Jordan. Of course.'

Alice did look at him then. 'Um — I'm sorry, have we met before?'

'No, we haven't.'

He must have recognised her name then, she decided. She did write for the local newspaper, after all, *The Post,* and her by-line was becoming gratifyingly well known.

'Well, I'll award you full marks for the sheer ingenuity of your approach.' His one eyebrow lifted, completely independently of the other. Alice stared at it, mesmerised. She'd never actually seen that before. She'd always believed it to be mere novel-speak. 'Nil, sadly, for your driving technique.'

'Sorry? What?' Had she heard him correctly?

'Oh, you didn't hear. I'll award you full marks — '

'Yes, I thought that's what you said,'

Alice rejoined. 'But what exactly do you mean? *The sheer ingenuity* — ?'

This time the other eyebrow lifted. Alice couldn't help but smile, somewhat testily. Did he think such facial contortions would intimidate her or something? Because they didn't.

'Oh, so once more you think it's funny, Ms Jordan.' His smile now outdid hers in testiness. 'Let's hope your insurance company is equally amused because my repair bill will most likely be — shall we say — substantial, if not hefty.'

Alice closed her eyes. There went her no claims bonus, conscientiously built up over several years.

'I assume you have all your details with you, your card?'

He still hadn't answered her question concerning the ingenuity of her approach. Nonetheless, she returned to her own car to fetch her briefcase. The damage to her Fiesta wasn't too serious; at least, she hoped not. It was difficult to assess with its nose still embedded in the Ferrari. She sneaked a glance back at the driver. She had to admit he was an impressive figure of a man; almost as impressive as his beloved car. With hair the colour of a raven's wing and eyes like a brooding sky, plus a build that most other men would envy, he was unarguably someone to be reckoned with.

She pulled from her case one of the cards that she always carried with her and wrote all the details he would need on the back, then strode back to him. He was engaged in the task of separating — well, maybe more accurately disentangling — the two cars. He seemed to manage it without much effort at all.

'Just make sure yours starts,' he commanded. 'The front's a bit dented but I don't think it's damaged the engine.'

Alice got back into her car and turned the ignition key. Sure enough, it fired up straight away.

'I'd say you've got off pretty lightly.

Okay — well, I'll be in touch. We have a few matters to discuss, I'm sure you'll agree.'

While Alice was digesting the implications of that final remark, he climbed into his Ferrari, started the engine, revved it a couple of times and without another word, moved off. Clearly, the damage to his car wasn't serious either, and even the dent didn't look so bad now. So what on earth had all the fuss been about?

'Hey!' Alice called. 'Just a minute. What's your name?' But she was too late. Within seconds, the car was a red dot in the distance. His final words blazed back at her. *Matters to discuss? What matters?* His insurance company would sort out —

Oh, no. She groaned out loud. Not Dominic Falconer. It couldn't have been him. Not even she could be that unlucky.

★   ★   ★

Trying to convince herself that she was wrong and the man she'd just driven into couldn't possibly be Dominic Falconer, Alice drove into the centre of the moderately-sized town of Chelmleigh and pulled into the car park of the building that housed the offices and printing presses of *The Post*. She went straight to the editorial room which, to her relief, was empty. She desperately needed a few minutes to herself after the stress of the past half hour. She certainly didn't want any witnesses to her pulling her hair out.

'Darn it,' she yelled to the empty room, 'damned Ferrari drivers.' She furiously tucked in the oversized T-shirt which she invariably wore to camouflage breasts that she considered too large, and then energetically tightened the belt of her jeans, smoothing them down over hips that were nicely curved before shakily re-applying lipstick to a mouth that was sufficiently pink and luscious to really need no further embellishment. She was in the process of dragging a brush through her shoulder length, honey-blonde hair when Neil, her editor, called from his office. She hadn't realised he was there. Good grief, had he heard her yelling?

'Bad hair day?' He asked the question with more than a touch of irony.

He'd heard her, then. Alice grinned sheepishly at him.

'You could say that.' Should she tell him about her morning's encounter? Maybe no, not yet, at any rate. She'd find out first whether it was indeed Dominic Falconer.

'Well, I've got plenty to keep you occupied, so get over it.' He looked down at his note pad. 'I've fixed you two interviews for this morning. The first is with a chap called Reynolds. He's heading the review on the closure of the hospital. Find out what's going on with that. Our readers will want to know. Next, I've arranged for you to interview someone who's setting off on a walk for charity . . . Then there's an art exhibition at the library; we'll need photos of that, so take Martin. Can you bring in your note pad? There's a couple more things for you to see to — '

'Working all night then, am I?'

He grinned at her. 'Not quite.'

She grinned back. For all Neil's demanding ways, he and Alice were good friends, and just lately they seemed to have been growing closer. Alice wasn't altogether sure how she felt about that. Apart from the fact that Neil was forty to her twenty-eight, she'd always been strictly against embarking upon any sort of relationship with a work colleague, let alone an employer. If something did start up and then went wrong, where would that leave her regarding her job?

Yet she sensed that just one word from her would have Neil asking her out. There was a certain look in his eye, now and then. And she did like him. But she also loved her work. Journalism had been the only thing she'd ever wanted to do, right from the time when she was fourteen and had helped edit and run the school's weekly news bulletin. She hadn't been able to believe her luck when, upon leaving school with nothing out of the ordinary in exam passes, *The Post* had agreed to take her on.

From that day, she'd devoted herself to acquiring the necessary skills and to her gratification was fast becoming one of the paper's most prolific and controversial, as well as the most read, reporter, according to a recent poll that the newspaper had run. However, she couldn't deny being attracted to Neil. He was very good-looking with his fair hair, blue eyes and engaging grin. Heaps better looking, in fact, than the man with the Ferrari.

★ ★ ★

But, despite her non-stop work, she couldn't drive from her head the images of the man she'd run into. If he *had* been Dominic Falconer — and the more she repeated his words to herself, the more convinced she became that it was him — then she wouldn't be surprised to see him at the offices, demanding to see her, insisting that she halt her campaign against him.

Eventually, she told herself to stop being so paranoid. She'd go and see Zoe after work; talk about it, get it off her chest. Zoe had the knack of restoring whatever problem Alice had to its proper perspective. Nothing seemed to faze her friend; she took all of life's irritations in her stride. Alice didn't know what she'd do without her. They'd been close friends since schooldays, so close that Alice was godmother to Zoe's three-year-old daughter, Imogen.

She rang Zoe's doorbell with two swift stabs. Zoe didn't always answer the door if she wasn't expecting anyone, and this was their agreed signal.

Zoe opened the door, Imogen in her arms.

'Auntie Alice,' Imogen cried with an

angelic smile, holding out her arms.

'Hello, my darling,' Alice responded, taking the little girl from Zoe.

'Faithless hussy,' Zoe muttered darkly to the back of her daughter's head. Her smile at her friend, however, was warm and welcoming. 'So how are you?' Her gaze went beyond Alice to the Fiesta. 'Oh dear, is that a dent I see? What happened?'

'I had an accident.'

'Well, I can see that.'

'I hit the back of a Ferrari.'

'Wow! You don't do things by halves, do you? Mind you, if you're going to hit something, you might as well make it something worth hitting.'

'Don't,' Alice groaned. 'I've waved bye-bye to my no-claims bonus.'

'What's a Fewawi, Auntie Alice?'

'An exorbitantly expensive vehicle, my sweet,' Alice told her god-daughter. 'Why anyone would pay that much for a lump of metal is beyond me,' she grumbled.

'Coffee?' Zoe gave a wicked grin.

'Sounds as if you need the caffeine.'

'Yes, please.' While Zoe busied herself with the percolator, Alice filled her in on what had happened that morning. She also gave a blow-by-blow description of the car's owner. 'He was horrible, Zoe, So sure of himself, so rude. Practically called me an airhead. I can't stand people who flaunt their wealth like that.'

'Not much point having it if you don't flaunt it, love,' Zoe murmured.

'Then I told him my name and he — he more or less accused me of hitting him deliberately. Called it an *ingenious approach*. Zoe,' she burst out, 'I've got this awful feeling it was — '

'Dominic Falconer? Your description fits him to a tee.'

2

Alice clapped a hand to her forehead. 'I knew it. Oh, Zoe, what am I going to do? He thinks I ran into his car on purpose.' Indignation coloured her cheeks pink. 'This will ruin everything. He won't listen to a word I say now. And what's more, I've given him the perfect stick to beat me with. A brainless, incompetent woman driver. What would she know about anything? Why would he — or anyone else, come to that — take any notice of my views after this?'

'Alice, love, calm down. Don't you think the tone of your article — providing he's read it, of course, but it does sound as if he has — might already have alienated him sufficiently that he wouldn't heed your arguments anyway? Whatever you've done since.'

'I suppose,' Alice grudgingly conceded.

'Maybe I should have arranged an interview with him first. But it wouldn't have changed my opinion of what he's planning to do. I'd still have written the same things.'

'So you're no worse off, then, than if you hadn't had the misfortune to run into the back of his car. Either way, he probably wouldn't listen to your arguments, and I'm sure he doesn't think you ran into him deliberately.'

'Oh, yes, he does. At least, that's what he implied.' She repeated word for word what Dominic had said.

'Hmm,' Zoe said thoughtfully. 'Well, you'll just have to convince him he's wrong on that.'

'How on earth will I convince him?'

'Oh, I'm sure you'll think of something. I can't imagine there are many men who'd be able to resist the allure of those green eyes, those dimpled cheeks, that hourglass figure.' Zoe grinned mischievously at her friend.

'But why didn't he say who he was? He must've realised I didn't know.'

'Well, if you're right and he does think you ran into him deliberately, he would have assumed you knew him. And I have to say, Alice, I am surprised you didn't recognise him. His photo was in *The Telegraph* a while ago, some big merger he's working on. And didn't you use a photo of him?'

'Well, yes, but it was an old one — and I didn't see the other one. How old would you say he is?'

'Mid-thirties, I would think.'

'Well, the picture I used must have been taken at least ten years ago. He didn't look much more than twenty-two or three. Mind you, it was blurred.'

'Actually, I saw him myself, coming out of the newsagent's last week, and he was carrying a newspaper, now I come to think of it. How much do you bet it was *The Post*?'

'I didn't know he was even here.' Alice groaned. 'Why didn't you tell me? I would have been prepared, then — I mean, a stranger driving a Ferrari? I might have guessed it would be him,' she argued irrationally.

'And how on earth would that have helped?' Zoe cried. 'You'd still have run into him, wouldn't you?'

'Just a minute.' Alice eyed her suspiciously. 'You've never met him either. How can you be sure it *was* him?'

'Mrs Cooper was with me. She told me who he was. She seems to know everybody. She's amazing.'

'So, he has read my piece,' Alice said grimly. 'It was on the front page.'

★ ★ ★

Once Zoe had confirmed that the man in the Ferrari was indeed Dominic Falconer, Alice knew she had to do something pretty quickly. He must have decided to stay on in the town. But why? As much as she loved Chelmleigh, it was hardly the hub of the business world. And his wretched plans hadn't even been passed yet. So what was keeping him here? Unless — her mind went into overdrive — he was here to grease a few palms, to make sure his plans went through, despite any local opposition. Having met him, she wouldn't be at all surprised if that was the truth of the matter. And if he had indeed read her article, maybe he wanted to be here to fight her campaign personally, face to face?

In which case, it was time to act decisively, to show him exactly how much opposition he faced. To force him to abandon his plans, forthwith. With this in mind, Alice resolved to hold a protest meeting in the town hall for two days' time, hoping against hope that it wasn't at too short notice for people. Luckily, the hall was available, so she plastered hastily-made posters all around the town, and phoned everyone she could think of. The response she received was depressingly half-hearted, but, at least the majority of people she spoke to agreed to attend.

She'd already carried out some research on Dominic for her article and decided it would be extremely unwise to underestimate him. He wielded considerable power, as well as possessing several influential friends, some in very high places. She'd even read that he had dined at 10 Downing Street.

Alice was under no illusions. He was a formidable opponent, and a series of articles in a local paper were not going to be enough to stop him. She had to galvanise local people into action. It was the only way.

However, by quarter to eight on the evening in question, Alice wasn't at all confident of the success of her protest meeting. A few people dribbled in, but in nothing like the numbers she'd hoped for. By eight o'clock, when the meeting was scheduled to start, the hall was only half-full. Still, beggars couldn't be choosers, she decided; at least some had arrived. She could have been facing an empty hall.

She saw Mrs Cooper come in, then Zoe, Richard, and Richard's younger brother, Sam. Thank Heavens for that.

She was relying on Zoe's support. Richard's, she wasn't so sure of. He avoided her smiling gaze, his mouth drawn into a tight line of what looked like disapproval. She knew his building firm was hoping to get the work once Dominic's plans were passed. By all accounts, they needed it. So she supposed she couldn't blame him for being less than enthusiastic.

She was surprised to see Sam, though; he was only just twenty, and she wouldn't have thought he'd be that interested in local affairs. Still, she was immensely grateful for whatever support she could get. The more people who turned out, the sooner Dominic Falconer would realise that the community didn't want his huge leisure centre spoiling their town.

A ripple of excitement suddenly went round the hall and every head swivelled to look at the latest arrival.

Dominic Falconer himself strode in.

Alice didn't know whether to be pleased or dismayed. She'd wondered if he might turn up, but had dismissed the prospect as unlikely. She'd been sure that Mr High and Mighty wouldn't choose to mix with the hoi polloi. How wrong she'd been.

Without as much as a glance at her, he took a seat right at the back, whereupon he drew a sheet of paper out of his jacket pocket and proceeded to study it. He was oblivious to the buzz of interest which his entrance had provoked. Typical! Alice snorted. His snubbing of her was quite deliberate, she was positive. He wanted her to feel insignificant; not worthy of a second look. In other words, to show her she couldn't win the battle. Not against someone like him. The trouble was, his tactics were working. She felt her confidence begin to waver.

Since speaking to Zoe, she'd carried out some further research and learned that he was self-made, extremely rich, and a financial wizard to boot. He had gathered together a vast portfolio of investments, and he had indeed been a regular visitor to 10 Downing Street in the capacity of some sort of advisor. He was currently expanding his business interests, of which he already had many, into the property development market and the proposed leisure centre was just one of several projects that he was involved with. He was well on the way to building himself an empire, her source had told her. Falcon Enterprises, the name of his company, had submitted a planning application and from what she'd heard the council were keen for it to happen. Alice was equally as keen to show him — as well as the council — that the residents of Chelmleigh were one hundred percent against it. However, judging by the numbers that had turned up tonight, her prospects of doing that were pretty low.

To her relief, she saw Neil slip in. He spotted Dominic immediately and took a seat on the far side of the hall. Alice smiled. It was a clear demonstration of his support. Or, of course — her confidence wavered again — it could be that Neil was simply embarrassed about sitting near to the man against whom his paper was waging a campaign.

Deciding that she could put it off no longer, Alice walked to the middle of the stage. She was trembling with nervousness. This was the first time she'd done something like this.

'G-good evening,' she haltingly began, 'and thank you for coming. I'm — I'm Alice Jordan, I work for *The Post*. I'm sure that some of you will have read my article about the application for planning consent to construct a leisure centre here in our town and the battle we face to try and stop it.'

Her gaze was drawn irresistibly to Dominic. This time he met it, unsmilingly — although she did detect a flicker of some expression in his eyes. Could it be uncertainty, she wondered? It seemed unlikely.

'Brookner's Wood, as I'm sure everyone knows, has been sold, along with the surrounding 150 acres of

farmland, to one Dominic Falconer
— who is with us this evening.' All
heads once again swivelled to look at
the man in question, who politely nodded
in acknowledgement of the interest in
him, his expression untroubled.

Alice's lips tightened. Did nothing faze
him? The arrogant beast! Her resolve to
stop him in his tracks strengthened, as
did her voice. 'He will have to fell this
ancient woodland as well as remove a
few dozen hedgerows . . . '

The audience had begun to murmur.
Several shook their heads. Alice's spirits
rose at this discernible sign of people's
disapproval. As a result, her voice
steadied.

'As I'm sure you are well aware,
Brookner's Wood is the home of the last
small group of red squirrels in this
region. If the wood is destroyed they,
too, will disappear, as will a multitude
of other valuable wildlife species and
plants. To stop this wholesale destruction — ' she felt Dominic's gaze searing
her skin — 'I have approached the

council for a preservation order upon the woodland, in particular the ancient oak trees.'

The murmur of voices grew, from a buzz to a roar. Dominic's expression had hardened, his eyes narrowing into slits.

'And,' she raised her voice in order to be heard over the uproar, 'I'm extremely hopeful of obtaining it — '

'Maybe some of us would rather have the leisure centre,' a man suddenly shouted out.

'Yes!' Someone else joined in. 'Think about what a development like that will do for Chelmleigh, the money it will bring into the town, the jobs it will create . . . '

Within seconds, the noise had become overwhelming, completely drowning out Alice's attempted protests. Throughout it all, Dominic sat, smug and silent. And no wonder. The meeting descended into chaos. A few hardy souls attempted to back Alice, but many more didn't. She did manage to shout that there was a petition at the door if they wished to sign it, and in the newspaper office, but she didn't hold out much hope of any worthwhile results. Not if the response she'd received here was typical.

Dominic left without having uttered a word. He hadn't needed to. The audience had put his case for him. Nobody seemed bothered by the prospect of increased traffic, the pollution, or the destruction of wildlife.

'Never mind,' Neil reassured her as people were leaving. 'You brought the whole issue out into the open. No-one can say they weren't warned. I'll do an editorial on it.'

'Alice!' It was Zoe. 'Well done. Good try.'

'Not good enough, obviously,' Alice replied bitterly. There was no sign of Zoe's husband. 'Richard's gone, has he?'

Zoe looked uncomfortable. 'Yes, he had to get home.'

'I'm just surprised he came. What did you do to get him here? Threaten to go on strike? Sorry,' Alice apologised, seeing her friend's discomfiture. 'Is he very angry with you for supporting me? That is, I presume you are supporting me?'

'Of course I am. He's a bit annoyed, but he knows I have a mind of my own. Have you heard the latest, by the way?'

Zoe was trying to change the subject, Alice realised. 'No. What?'

'Dominic Falconer has bought a house.'

'So? Even the Devil has to live somewhere.' Alice smiled wryly.

'Well, yes — but not here in Chelmleigh.'

'Good!' Alice tossed her head. 'That means he'll have to live amongst the chaos he's hell-bent on creating.'

'He won't. He's only gone and bought Chelmleigh Manor — well away from the site of the centre, and all the noise and mess.'

Alice's smile was grim. 'Well, he should be perfectly at home there. From what I've heard, it's been colonised by the town's entire population of rats and mice. It has been empty now for almost two years, after all.'

'He intends to restore it to its former glory, apparently. He's commissioned a firm of top London designers — '

Alice snorted. 'Why am I not surprised about that piece of information?'

'However,' Zoe stressed, 'he's let it be known that he's going to be employing local craftsmen — '

'Supposing we have any, of course,' Alice rudely interrupted.

' — and decorators,' Zoe went on as if Alice hadn't spoken, 'for the actual work on the house as well as the leisure centre — if and when that's built.'

'It's nothing short of bribery,' Alice cried. ''Let me build my monstrosity and I'll keep you all in work for months to come.' What a creep!'

3

A whole week passed before Alice encountered Dominic Falconer again. She was talking to Mrs Cooper, who did seem to be one of the few hardy souls who were on Alice's side.

Alice was grumbling. 'Dominic Falconer's got absolutely no regard for other people's opinions — '

'Any more than *you* have,' a voice said from behind her, 'judging by the tone of your latest article.'

Alice whirled, and catapulted straight into the subject of her complaints. 'Oh, it's you,' she muttered darkly.

'You do have the most unfortunate habit of colliding with stationary objects, don't you?' Dominic grunted, visibly winded from the force of the impact. 'Fortunately, this time, there's no damage done — if you discount a bruised toe.' He glanced pointedly down at his right foot, where Alice could quite clearly see the imprint of her heel on the front of his shoe.

'What are you doing here? Oh, don't tell me — making the most of the peace and tranquillity of the place before you destroy it for good. Which leads me on to my next question. Why would you choose to live here? I thought people like you kept well away from the damage that they inflict.'

His eyes turned to steel. 'It's a pity that you're so out of sympathy with the majority of the residents here, Ms Jordan. Surely, even you must have realised by now that they actually want what I'm proposing. They believe it will be a valuable amenity. Fortunately, your editor understands this.'

Alice had been furious when she'd read Neil's promised editorial. It had sounded as if he actually supported the scheme. She'd felt utterly betrayed, and had had no compunction in saying so.

'Betrayed you?' He'd looked surprised, if not a little hurt. 'I reported events as they happened. Wasn't that what you wanted?'

Alice hadn't had an answer for that. If she'd said 'no', it would have sounded as if she had expected him to compromise his principles for the sake of supporting her, and she knew better than anyone that Neil would never agree to that.

'In answer to your question,' Dominic was saying calmly, 'I happen to like the area and I happen to like the people who inhabit it — with the exception of the odd one, obviously.'

Alice glowered at him. He obviously meant her.

'Why don't you listen to your readers, Ms Jordan, and abandon this futile campaign? You're heavily outnumbered.' He paused, a tiny smile flirting with his lips. 'Tell me, how many signatures did you collect on your petition? That would be a sure guide to public opinion.'

'Enough,' she snapped.

'Really.' Dominic brought his eyebrow into play.

Again, Alice glared at him. Blasted man!

'Because I heard that you only managed to dredge up half a dozen.'

'And who told you that?'

'Does it matter? I know.'

Alice eyed him. 'You've been to the newspaper reception desk and looked, haven't you?'

'Is there any reason why I shouldn't have? It's there for anyone to sign.'

'I didn't mean *you*,' she blazed.

'Oh, didn't you? Well, rest easy, I didn't sign it.' His mouth twitched with amusement. 'I'm afraid that you'll need considerably more ammunition than that to persuade me to abandon my plans.' He tilted his head to one side and eyed her from beneath lowered lashes. 'You obviously haven't heard.'

'Heard what?'

'That I have the full backing of Chelmsleigh's MP, Christopher Bryant, as well as the support of the council's entire planning department.'

Alice snorted. 'I'm just surprised you

haven't enlisted the support of your crony, the Prime Minister. After all, you're on his dinner party guest list, so I've heard. And as for Chris Bryant, I'll just say his favourite position is straddling the fence. So, I wouldn't place too much faith in his word.'

She'd phoned Mr Bryant to ask his views on the construction of the leisure centre before writing her first article, and all he'd done was splutter and prevaricate, so that she'd ended up none the wiser as to his opinion — although she'd hazarded a pretty good guess. He was for the development.

'My, my,' Dominic murmured, 'you have been doing your research, haven't you?'

'It's my job.'

'Evidently.' He studied her for a long moment. Then, 'Tell me, who did you approach about getting a preservation order on the oak trees? It's been puzzling me somewhat, because, you see, I can't find anyone who knows anything about your request. Chris certainly doesn't know.'

He'd rumbled her. He knew she'd been — what was the phrase? — economical with the truth. She'd have to brazen it out.

'I'm seeing someone next week.'

'Oh! So you haven't actually approached anyone yet?'

'No.' She gnawed at her bottom lip — a sure sign, did Dominic but know it, that she was apprehensive.

'You'll give yourself a sore lip if you go on doing that,' he admonished. 'I've noticed it's a particular habit of yours whenever you get nervous.'

So, Mr Smarty Pants had even sussed that out. Oh, how she hated him. Him and his infernal eyebrow.

'Look,' he said suddenly, 'why don't you and I go somewhere and talk the whole thing through? Just the two of us, over a drink. Maybe we could reach some sort of compromise that will make everyone happy.'

'And where would you suggest we go,

Mr Falconer — '

'Isn't it time you called me Dominic?'

She ignored that. ' — *Mr* Falconer,' she repeated. 'To Hell, maybe? Dangerous, that, though, they might not let you out again.'

Once more, his lips quirked with amusement. Her fury intensified at the sight. 'There's something I really ought to explain.' She leaned slightly towards him. 'You are the very last person I'd drink with. And what sort of compromise do you think we could reach? You either abandon your plans — totally — or you have a real fight on your hands.'

'Are you sure you want to do this?' His eyes had softened as he spoke. 'Alone?' Something that could have been sympathy showed upon his face.

She stiffened. How dare he pity her? Her determination strengthened. She'd show him. Alone or not, she would fight him every inch of the way.

'I won't be alone.' Alice lifted her chin. 'In time, people will come round to my view — when they see the extent of your scheme.' She'd already inspected the plans and had been horrified at their dimensions. It wouldn't be far off a Center Parcs development — right on people's doorsteps. Of course they'd come round when they saw that.

'Ah, but time is something you don't have.'

A sense of foreboding filled her then. 'What do you mean?'

'Chris Bryant is going to rush the application through personally. He and the council are keen to get the work started and thereby show a reduction in the number of unemployed — '

'Excuse me.'

Alice turned. She'd completely forgotten Mrs Cooper was standing there.

'I don't want to interfere, but I've been and had a look at the plans and I don't see why the complex couldn't be built in and around the woodland. You know, incorporate the trees somehow. That way, we'd get to keep them — or, at least, a number of them — and also reap the benefits that such an amenity would offer.'

Alice was aghast. 'I thought you were against it?'

'I'm trying to see both sides, Alice. Don't let your desire to preserve the environment in its entirety blind you to the wellbeing of the town and its residents as a whole.'

'But even if we keep the trees — the squirrels, the badgers, they wouldn't stay. Not with all the noise and mess of a building site. No, we might still have our trees but there'd be nothing living in them!'

Oh dear — now she was starting to sound shrill, she realised in horror.

'I'm sure they'd come back,' the old lady said. 'Animals are very resilient; they have to be.'

'No!' Alice could hear her voice rising again. Now she was sounding hysterical. Dominic would be sure to pick up on that. She was right.

'Aren't you getting a bit carried away over this, Ms Jordan?'

'Well, somebody has to get carried away, Mr Falconer, or nothing will be done about it. We'll have no country-side left to speak of if developers like you are allowed to ride roughshod over everyone. No, I won't give up.'

She fell silent, debating the wisdom of asking her next question. Oh, blow it! Nothing ventured, nothing gained.

'Tell me. Exactly how much have you had to pay Chris Bryant to rush your application through? A thousand pounds? Several thousand pounds? A million? I think the people of Chelmleigh have a right to know. After all, they will be the ones most affected by your underhand dealings.'

'Do be careful, dear,' Mrs Cooper hissed into Alice's ear. But it was too late for words of caution.

'I'll forget you said that, Ms Jordan,' Dominic rasped, 'even though I have a reliable witness — '

'Oh, I really wouldn't count on that, Mr Falconer,' Mrs Cooper said imme-diately. 'Alice and I have been friends for many years now. I would be extremely loath to do anything to jeopardise that.'

Dominic didn't respond to that declaration of loyalty. Neither did he remove his gaze from Alice.

Alice shivered. You could cut yourself on that look. Maybe she should rethink her course of action? Who knew what he'd be capable of if pushed too far? But someone had to fight for the woodland, she told herself, and who else would do it but her? And what could he do to her when all was said and done? He might closely resemble the Devil himself in looks, but he was a mere mortal — just like everyone else.

* * *

Just three weeks later, when Dominic Falconer moved into the renovated Chelmleigh Manor, Alice had to seriously question that judgment. She would have thought such a feat, considering the deplorable state the house had been in, would have been beyond anyone — even him. Clearly, she had been wrong.

But if he and his army of designers and decorators had been busy, so had Alice. She'd been tireless in her efforts to whip up support for her campaign. A few people had pledged their help, but in nothing like the numbers she needed to make the planning department take notice and so stop the construction of the new complex.

Even Zoe was showing signs of wavering. When Alice had asked her why, she'd prevaricated. 'We-ell . . . '

'It's Richard, isn't it? He's talked you out of it.'

'In a way. I'm sorry, Alice, but he is my husband. And to be fair, Dominic has restored the Manor so well, I'm sure he'd do the same sort of job on the leisure centre. And then, of course — '

'Richard's business needs the work,' Alice finished bleakly for her.

'Well, yes,' Zoe agreed.

'So I'm more or less on my own in

this,' Alice stated.

'I'm sorry, Alice — '

'Don't be. You have to think of Richard and your own livelihood.'

'There's some talk in the town that Dominic is planning on retaining a lot of the trees.'

But Alice knew that wouldn't make a scrap of difference. The heart would have been cut out of the woodland and its valuable wildlife would have left. The ecological balance of the area would have been destroyed — in all likelihood, for good.

If things looked bad for Alice in that moment, they were about to get a whole lot worse. One morning, Neil called her into his office.

'I want you to go and interview Falconer at the Manor. He's been there now for ten days or so, so he should be well and truly settled in. Fine out how he's effected the transformation so speedily; get some photos of the interior. He's worked miracles, apparently.'

'Huh! Don't you mean his team of minions have?' Alice snapped with contempt. 'He's had up to forty people working there. I doubt if he's picked up a brush himself. Anyway, there's no way I'm doing an interview with him.'

'Oh, yes, you are, Alice.' Neil sounded uncharacteristically firm.

What was happening to everyone? Alice agonised. They were all deserting her. Even Mrs Cooper was in two minds about the development, despite her staunch defence during Alice's stand-off with Dominic. 'I've heard he once took someone to court for a lot less than you just said — and won,' the old lady had muttered warningly.

Alice had ignored her words. Instead, she'd met Dominic's look fearlessly, and had only just stopped herself from cheering when he'd said, 'I'll see you around, Ms Jordan, I'm sure,' and then walked away.

Well, round one to her, she thought — or was it round two?

'Has he been getting at you, too?' she

demanded now furiously of Neil.

Neil looked astonished. 'If you mean Falconer — '

'Obviously I do.'

Neil did have the grace to look a little shame-faced. 'We did have a chat the other evening over a pint in The Boar's Head.'

'I see.' Alice sniffed. 'Put *his side of things*, did he? How many pints did it take? Two? Three?'

Neil's face paled alarmingly. Alice flinched. Maybe she'd overstepped the mark there?

'It wasn't like that.' His tone was one of quiet determination. 'I'm not open to bribery — by anyone.' And he stared unwaveringly until she dropped her gaze.

But Alice, being Alice, couldn't let the subject drop. 'I thought better of you; Neil. I never dreamed you'd share a drink with someone who's threatening our whole way of life — '

'Oh, do stop dramatising everything, Alice. He's not threatening our whole way of life. He just wants to build a leisure centre.'

Alice glowered at him.

'And, as an editor, I have to remain impartial.'

'Huh! You must be the only editor in the country who does then,' she growled defiantly.

'I'm not arguing with you over this, Alice. I want that interview and you are going to do it.' He didn't actually add 'if you want to keep your job', but the implication was there.

'But I can't!' she cried. 'Surely you can see that?'

'Yes, you can.'

'How can I oppose him over his plans on the one hand and go and interview him on the other? It'd be ridiculous! Hypocritical.' Something occurred to her. 'Of course, if I can also question him on those plans — '

'No. I want this to be a feature solely on his renovation. Something that will appeal to our female readers.'

'But, Neil — '

'Alice, no. Every reader will know of your opposition to him; it will lend spice to the article. Get people buying the paper just to read what you say to him and what he says to you.'

'Spice!' Alice was outraged. He wanted to exploit her feelings just to entertain his readers.

'Well, maybe spice is the wrong word. Let's say excitement.'

Alice stormed from his office, every nerve in her body jangling. The man was a chauvinist. How could she ever have been attracted to him? She stomped back to her desk and, once there, punched out the number of Chelmleigh Manor on her mobile phone. If she had to do it, she'd do it immediately and get it over with. She wasn't going to waste her time worrying. *Worrying?* She snorted. She wasn't worried. She was more than equal to the task of interviewing Dominic Falconer, hateful as it would be. As she'd already assured herself more than once, he was only a man, after all.

She heard the phone ringing out and was bracing herself for the indignity of having to ask the man himself for an interview when an attractively husky female voice answered 'Chelmleigh Manor. Belinda Falconer speaking.'

Belinda Falconer? Who the blue blazes was Belinda Falconer?

'Um — yes,' Alice began haltingly. Not for a second had she considered that Dominic was married. In fact, nothing she had read or been told about him had ever suggested such a thing.

'I — I'd like to speak to Mr Falconer, please.'

'Of course. Whom shall I say is calling?'

'Alice Jordan. I work for the — '

'Yes,' the voice abruptly cut her off, 'I know who you work for.'

Alice could almost feel the shards of ice slicing down the phone line. She heard the woman say, 'Dominic. Alice Jordan is on the phone.'

The phone must have been wrenched

from the woman's hand, so swiftly did Dominic speak. 'What do you want?'

Clearly, he hadn't forgotten their last encounter and the things she'd accused him of. She swallowed. Mind you, he hadn't denied it, had he?

'I've been instructed — ' she didn't want him to think she was doing this of her own free will — 'to come to the Manor and conduct an interview with you, Mr Falconer. Would now be convenient? I could be there in ten minutes.'

The silence on the other end of the phone lasted so long that Alice began to think he'd hung up. Just as she was on the point of doing the same thing, however, he spoke. 'I presume Neil is the one who issued the instruction?'

Mutely, Alice fumed. So they were on first name terms were they? Neil hadn't mentioned that. There was no mistaking the delight in Dominic's voice. He was enjoying this. He knew full well how much she'd hate having to ask if she could come and see him.

It was Alice's turn to stay silent.

'He didn't mention anything about this the other evening. Did he tell you we had a drink together and a — long chat?'

Self-satisfaction oozed from the phone. Alice held it away from her ear and glared at it.

'He did, yes. He thinks our female readers would be *fascinated* — ' she stressed the word, ladling on the sarcasm — 'to hear in your own words all about your renovation. With photographs, of course.'

'Well, yes. That would be fine.'

Alice closed her eyes in vexation. She'd been hoping he might refuse. Then Neil wouldn't have had a leg to stand on. She tried another tack.

'Of course, if you would prefer someone else to do the interview, I would perfectly understand — '

'No. You'll do nicely, Ms Jordan. Shall we say ten minutes' time, then? Good.' She was positive he was grinning. He knew he had the better of her. 'The photographs will reassure local people of my intention to construct the leisure centre in the most sympathetic way possible, thus ensuring it will blend in with its surroundings.'

'How will a brand new building blend in with what was a long-established piece of woodland, no matter how *sympathetically* — ' she sarcastically emphasised the word — 'it is constructed?'

'When you see how I have restored Chelmleigh Manor so that it looks as it would have done centuries ago, I'm sure you will concede that the same thing can be achieved with the new.'

'Yes, but you had the original house to work with.'

'Quite, but with the use of reclaimed materials, such as bricks and timber, buildings can be made to look ancient.'

'I'm sure they can be, but your plans still mean the destruction of a valuable and irreplaceable piece of countryside. I'm afraid I can't see — '

'You're afraid?' he scoffed. 'I very

much doubt that. Fear certainly didn't stop you accusing me of corruption — and,' his voice took on a menacing tone, as well as dropping a level, 'believe me, it should have done.'

Alice held her breath. 'Are you threatening me?'

'No. I have decided that you spoke in the heat of the moment, as well as the bitter knowledge of certain defeat.'

'Certain defeat? I won't be defeated!' she began indignantly. Oh, for goodness' sake. She was getting nowhere. The wretched man was like a block of concrete. Immovable. Intransigent. Nothing she said made any difference to him. The only way forward was some sort of action. She'd get this interview over with, and then — well, she'd come up with something, she was sure. She had to. She couldn't afford to fail. He had to be stopped.

'Will eleven o'clock suit you?' Her voice was unbelievably calm, despite the turmoil raging inside her. She congratulated herself on her self-restraint.

'I can let you have half an hour.'

Once again, Alice had to conceal her emotions. Who did he think he was with this detestable display of arrogance? *I can let you have half an hour*, indeed. 'Maybe I could talk to Mrs Falconer as well?'

Dominic didn't respond.

'Get a woman's viewpoint on the restoration work.'

'Certainly.'

4

Alice swung her car through the gates of the Manor and accelerated up the twisting driveway. She was still seething about what she was being forced to do, but even in the midst of that she could see the excellence of the work that had been done on the exterior of the beautiful Queen Anne house. If the inside was its equal — ? She braked sharply in a swirl of gravel; Martin, the Post's photographer, pulled up in his own car behind her.

'Wow!' he exclaimed as he climbed from his car. 'And all in — what? A month or so?'

'Actually it's only taken him three weeks,' Alice muttered grudgingly.

'You have to admit, the man's got taste as well as expertise.'

Alice wasn't about to admit anything, and certainly not to someone who could well be at her side — depending on how long he took over the photographs — while she interviewed Dominic. Who knew what Martin might say? The last thing she wanted, or needed, was for Dominic to know she admired his work.

The front door opened and a woman stood there. 'Mrs Falconer?' Alice asked. She had resolved to be polite, in spite of the manner in which the woman had spoken to her on the phone. And in spite of the way in which she was regarding Alice right now. Alice scanned the ground around her. Where was the stone that she had supposedly crawled out from under?

She looked up again to find Belinda Falconer holding out a hand, her sapphire eyes icy, her lips tightly drawn. 'Yes. You must be Alice Jordan.'

Again, the tone of her voice suggested Alice was someone to be avoided at all costs. Alice felt her hackles rise. However, as much as she was tempted to ignore it, she forced herself to take the proffered hand. It felt every bit as cool as the woman's gaze. Alice couldn't stop herself from looking down at it. Three large diamonds flashed back at her, as well as a broad gold band, also diamond-studded. How flashy. And how unsurprising. Of course Dominic Falconer would cover his wife in jewels. She was just amazed they weren't also glittering in her ears and around her throat.

'Yes.' Alice managed to hide her scorn. 'And this is Martin Regis, the photographer.'

Belinda bestowed a gracious, warm smile upon Martin. 'Please, come in.' Alice, she pointedly ignored.

Undaunted, Alice stepped inside and found herself in a black and white tiled hallway as large as her entire flat, with space left over for an extra bathroom. It contained an elegant Adam fireplace and several pieces of fine antique furniture. A pale stone staircase curved upward to a galleried landing. Taste-wise, Alice had to admit, it was faultless.

Belinda flung open a door to the left and led them into what was clearly a library, rows of books covering every inch of wall space. Alice would bet he'd bought them by the yard. Nobody could really own this number of books, could they? The only break in this ostentatious display was another fireplace, before which was set a leather Chesterfield sofa and two winged armchairs. Dominic was sitting in one of the chairs. Seeing Alice enter, he got to his feet.

'Dominic, Ms Jordan and Mr Regis. If you'll excuse me I'll go and rustle up some coffee.'

Alice watched her leave. She was every inch the lady of the manor. Slender, shapely, and dressed in what was unmistakably a designer dress, she was lovely, if you liked ice queens. Alice didn't.

'If you'd both like to take a seat?' Dominic waved Alice towards the other chair. She took it.

'If you don't mind,' Martin put in,

'I'll take the photographs first. I've got another assignment to go to.'

'Yes, of course,' Dominic agreed. 'I thought perhaps the hallway with its stone staircase — a rather uncommon feature — and then maybe a view of the drawing room?'

'I wondered about one of Mr and Mrs Falconer together, Martin. In the hall, then?'

She glanced towards Dominic for his consent, only to see an odd little smile quirking his mouth.

'Fine,' he agreed. 'I'm sure Belinda won't mind.'

The door opened and a short, stocky woman entered, followed closely by Belinda. The housekeeper, Alice presumed. She set a tray on a conveniently placed low table. It held a large coffee pot and cream and sugar, plus four cups and saucers.

'Belinda,' Dominic began. 'Ms Jordan wants a photograph of you and me together.'

Belinda looked surprised but pleased. 'Does she? Heavens.' She patted an already immaculate hairdo and smoothed the skirt of her designer dress.

'Perhaps you and your wife — ' Alice went on.

'Oh, dear.' Dominic gave another smile. 'Whatever gave you the idea that Belinda is my wife? She's my sister-in-law.'

'Oh. Um — sorry. I thought, you know, Mrs Falconer . . . ' Alice stumbled lamely to a halt.

'Quite. A not uncommon mistake.'

'Well,' Alice cleared her throat, 'could you and Mrs Falconer please return to the hall?'

'Do you know, I think maybe it should just be Dominic,' Belinda ventured. 'After all, it's been mainly Dominic's work, the restoration. I've only just arrived, and to claim half of the credit — '

'Fine.' Alice's tone was one of indifference. She just wanted the interview over with. Dominic had known full well the misapprehension she'd been labouring under. That's what the strange little smiles had been

61

for. He seemed to take a perverse delight in her mistakes.

Once the photos had been taken from every angle and Martin had left, Belinda also politely made her excuses. 'I have to go out now. I'm sorry.'

With just the two of them left alone, Alice felt nervous. Mainly because her accusation of bribery and corruption was echoing once more in her head. That, and his warning on the telephone a little while ago that she should have thought twice before making it. To occupy herself, she pulled out her tape recorder and set it on the table that sat between them.

'You don't mind, do you? I find it the most reliable way of doing things. No arguments afterwards about who said what or even if it was said at all.' Dominic nodded, so Alice switched the recorder on. As she did so, her hand knocked against her coffee cup, spilling some of the liquid onto the polished surface of the table.

'Oh, sorry. I'll just — ' She pulled a

paper tissue from her pocket and swiftly mopped it up. Unfortunately, it left a long streak behind it. Embarrassed, she rubbed harder.

'Leave it,' Dominic ordered. 'My word, you are accident-prone, Ms Jordan. Life must be an endless trial for you. How do you cope?'

Alice tightened her mouth but didn't respond. When she did speak, it was to say smoothly, 'So, perhaps you'd like to tell me about the restoration work. How you got started.'

'Well, I didn't get started. As I'm sure you realise. I employed an excellent team of interior designers, craftsmen and decorators. The designer was Chloe Donaghue; I'm sure you must have heard of her. She's very well known in the field of restoration work.'

Alice wasn't about to admit she didn't have the slightest idea who the woman was, so she just nodded.

'I find women are superior to men in the question of decor, don't you?'

'I wouldn't know,' Alice conceded.

'I've never lived with a man to — '

'Oh, have you not?'

There went that infernal eyebrow again. Alice simmered. It implied that he wasn't at all surprised that no man would take her on.

'And yet, you must be — what? Twenty-six? Seven?'

Again, Alice said nothing. There was no way she was going to tell him she was twenty-eight. It was none of his business. Not when he clearly had her down as a lonely, unloved spinster. Okay, so there was no current man in her life, but that didn't mean there never had been. She just hadn't yet met the one she wanted to spend the rest of her life with.

'Was it all in a very bad state when you bought it?' She waved her hand, indicating the house in general.

His mouth twitched. He was obviously amused by her refusal to reveal her age. 'Horrendous,' he admitted, grimacing. For the first time, he actually looked human. 'But nothing that a lot of hard work and the appropriate craftsmen — and women — haven't been able to put right, as you can see.'

'And, of course, unlimited wealth. One can do anything with that. Such extensive and expensive renovation would be well beyond the means, and pockets, of the average man, don't you agree?'

'Ah, but then, Ms Jordan,' he looked positively wolfish, 'I'm not the average man. As I would have thought you'd have learned by this time.' His smile possessed all the qualities of a very sharp blade. Smooth, but with a distinctly dangerous edge.

'No,' she muttered, 'you're not, are you, Mr Fal — '

'Oh, please, can't we leave the formalities behind? The name is Dominic, it's so much more friendly, don't you think? And if we're going to be seeing a lot of each other — '

'Seeing a lot of each other? Why would that be? If I had my way, our paths would never cross again.'

He sighed, somewhat melodramatically. 'Now, that would be a pity. For my part, I find our encounters stimulating — troublesome, maybe, and at times decidedly infuriating, but definitely stimulating. And I have to say, it would seem highly unlikely that we won't meet again as you're clearly intending to continue your campaign against me.'

'We won't meet face to face — if I have any say in the matter.'

He tilted his head to one side and subjected her to a quizzical stare. 'So how do you intend putting your case to me?' He steepled his fingers and rested them on his chin.

Alice decided to ignore that question. 'Tell me, don't you feel the smallest twinge of guilt that you've bought this house?'

He looked puzzled and, for the very first time in their acquaintance, slightly on the defensive. 'Why on earth should I feel guilty?'

She'd done it, she thought gleefully, promptly forgetting that she wasn't supposed to be discussing his leisure centre. She'd got him on the run. 'Well, as it's on the opposite side of the town to where your planned development will be, it won't be you that has to suffer the nuisance factor of it all, will it? The noise, the dust, the lorries passing all day long.'

His expression hardened. 'I was under the distinct impression, Ms Jordan, that this interview was to be about the house restoration and nothing else. So, shall we return to that subject, or do you wish me to terminate the interview?'

Alice had no option but to do as he said.

It wasn't until she was packing away her tape recorder again that Dominic said conciliatorily, 'I hope you got your car repaired okay.'

'Oh — yes. There wasn't much damage.'

'Good. I've submitted estimates for my repairs to my insurance company.

The damage wasn't as bad as it appeared; I'm sure you'll be relieved to hear that.'

''I'm sure you'll be relieved to hear that',' she mimicked Dominic's drawl sarcastically as she drove away. 'Of course I was relieved, you patronising man!' she cried, just as if he were there in the car with her. Mind you, it would still cost her her precious no-claims bonus.

Once back at her desk, she set about composing her article, making no bones about emphasising the vast amounts of money that Dominic Falconer must have spent on the renovation. She concluded the piece by pointing out that the new owner of Chelmleigh Manor had ensured his own peace and tranquillity by purchasing a house as far away from the predictable noise and sheer inconvenience of the new centre as he could possibly get.

'No, Alice,' Neil pronounced upon reading it. 'I didn't ask for a demolition report on Falconer.' Ruthlessly he started to wield his red pen. 'I asked for a write-up on his restoration. Now, using the suggestions I've written on it, go and re-do it. There's a good girl.'

Alice snatched the document up. 'Whose side are you on anyway, Neil?'

'I'm trying very hard to remain impartial.'

'From where I'm standing, it looks perilously like support for Falconer.'

'Well, you're wrong. There are an awful lot of people out there — our readers, remember? — who want this complex. If we alienate them by being too strong in our views against it, we'll lose them.'

'So it's all about numbers? How many papers we sell. We moderate our opinions to keep the readers happy. I thought you had more integrity.'

'I'll ignore that and just say, without our readership we go under. Is that what you want?' His colour had risen along with his anger. 'Look, this is ridiculous, you and I fighting about it. Let me buy you dinner; we can discuss all of this.'

Alice stared at him. 'You think buying me dinner will solve anything?'

'Well, yes — if we can talk it all over away from the office. I know having dinner with me won't influence you, Alice, but you have to understand, I'm simply trying to do my job and give both sides of the argument. That's what we do. Will you come?' His blue eyes gleamed at her.

'Oh, all right. I'd like that.' And she really would, she realised.

★　★　★

Alice was 15 minutes late for their rendezvous. 'Sorry, sorry,' she cried. 'Re-writing that piece took longer than I expected. Actually, Neil, I've had a brilliant idea for the campaign. It needn't involve the paper. It would be just me acting on my own . . . '

Neil groaned. 'Oh no. What now, Alice?'

'I could sell badges — you know. SAVE OUR WOOD badges. I could put all the money I make towards a fund to buy back the land from Dominic. The town's summer fete is only two weeks away: I could sell them there.'

Neil started to laugh, so loudly that other diners began to glance at them. 'Buy the land back? Do you have any idea how much that would cost?'

'Well — roughly.' The ideas were starting to come, thick and fast. 'I could organise other events — '

'You'd need to, and pretty damned smartly. They're rushing through the planning application.'

'I know, the great man himself told me.'

'So how will selling a few badges help?'

'I can only try.'

'Alice, Alice, you'd need a miracle.' He shook his head despairingly.

'Well, maybe I'll get one.'

'You also need the whole town on your side.'

'I have to try, Neil.'

'Take it from me, Falconer won't sell to you. He stands to make too much money from this. You're onto a loser, believe me.' He caught hold of her hands across the table. 'Give it up.'

'No.' She snatched her hands away. His gentle touch was doing strange things to her heartbeat, and she'd already decided that any sort of relationship between her and Neil was out of the question. There could be no future for them — not as long as she worked for him.

'You'll only get hurt if you go on fighting him. He's too powerful.'

'I have to try,' she repeated quietly. 'I have to.'

5

Somehow — she decided afterwards that the gods must have been smiling on her — Alice managed to get her badges ready. If past attendance levels were anything to go by, the fete was the perfect place to sell them. Even if she couldn't raise the funds, eventually, to buy back the land — and she was realising that Neil was right, she'd set herself an impossible task, even if she had the time — she could hopefully muster more support for her cause, and surely then Dominic Falconer would have to sit up and take notice of her viewpoint?

In fact, she wouldn't sell the badges; she'd give them away. Yes, that was a much better idea. Surely then, she'd be able to persuade people to wear them and Dominic wouldn't be able to ignore public opinion. Of course, she'd have to stand the cost of their manufacture herself, but if she managed to stop the development, it would have been worth it.

Her optimism intensified when the morning of the fete dawned hot and sunny. She'd managed to get one the many stalls that would be there, someone having cancelled at the last minute, and she quickly laid out her boxes of badges plus several photographs of Brookners Wood as it was now. Alongside these she placed various newspaper pictures, graphically portraying the destruction of rural sites around the country, sites that had once been just as beautiful as Brookners Wood.

Mrs Cooper was one of the first people to arrive at the fete. She made a beeline for Alice. 'What's this, then?'

'Badges, showing support for my campaign. Will you wear one?'

'Of course I will. It's a pity you don't have a bit more time.'

'I know. Do you think other people

will wear them?'

The old woman shrugged. 'Who can say?' She eyed Alice. 'The Falconers are on their way. He's been asked to judge the dog show, and she's doing the cakes and floral arrangements.' She glanced down at the photographs. 'I wonder what they'll make of all this?'

Alice shrugged, pretending a nonchalance she was far from feeling. 'They can make what they like of them. It's a free country.'

'Here come your friends, so I'll bid you a good day. Good luck with these.' She touched the badge, now pinned prominently on her jacket lapel.

Alice smiled a greeting at Zoe and Richard. Imogen was sitting in her buggy. Alice bent down and dropped a kiss upon her snub nose. 'And how's my angel?'

'Can I have one of dose, Auntie Alice?' The child pointed to the badge Alice was wearing. The bright colours had obviously attracted her gaze. Alice was trusting it would do the same with the Chelmleigh residents.

'Um — Imogen,' Richard cut in. 'I don't think that's a good idea, darling.'

'But I want one, Daddy.' Imogen began to pull a face.

'No, because Daddy doesn't agree with what it says.'

'Oh, Richard,' Zoe said. 'She's just a child.'

'You know Falconer's coming, Zoe. How will it look if the child of the man who's bidding to do the building work for him is wearing a SAVE OUR WOODS badge, for heaven's sake?'

'Oh, phooey,' Zoe laughed. 'He won't know who you are. I'll have one, Alice; he certainly won't know who *I* am.'

Nervously, Alice handed over a badge. She didn't want to be the cause of a domestic row. She needn't have worried, however. Richard simply looked daggers at his wife, snorted with disgust and walked away.

'Zoe, do you think you're being wise? I can see Richard's point.'

Zoe sighed. 'There's absolutely no

guarantee that his firm will even get the work — '

'Oh, look, there's Chris Bryant,' Alice interrupted. 'I need to have a word with him about the preservation order. It could be the one thing that stops the development. Mind the stall for me, Zoe, just for a minute?'

Ignoring Zoe's doubtful, 'Well, I don't know . . . ' Alice darted through the growing crowd, trying to keep the bulky figure of Chris Bryant in view, only to be brought to an abrupt halt by a large, immovable object.

Dominic Falconer.

'Oh, it's you again,' she muttered. The wretched man seemed to pop up everywhere.

He regarded her with amusement. 'Was that an apology that I heard?'

'Sorry,' she grudgingly replied.

'Tell me, do you deliberately pick me to collide with?' Gold glints appeared in the slate eyes.

'I didn't even see you there.'

'Just like the first time. You were

looking the other way then, as I recall.'

She ignored that jibe and hurried around him. She could still see Chris Bryant — just. 'Mr Bryant!' she called. 'Can I have a word?'

Chris Bryant swung round. A guarded look appeared on his face when he saw who it was calling him. 'Ah, Ms Jordan.'

'Um, I wondered about that preservation order — '

'I have to say, the chances of obtaining it aren't great. The council and the planning committee are staunchly behind Mr Falconer and his leisure centre. They feel that the area is sorely in need of such a facility. It will brings jobs and prosperity.'

'But surely, you have some influence. I mean, think of the wildlife that will be harmed, driven away. The red squirrels, the badgers — '

'They'll find somewhere else. They always do,' Mr Bryant said bluntly.

'Can I quote you on that?' Alice asked tartly. 'As our MP, who fought the election — and won his seat — on his promise to do all he could to protect the environment, local and nationwide?'

He flushed an unbecoming shade of puce. 'I'd rather you didn't. And if you did, I would, of course, fiercely deny it.'

'So, what you're telling me is that the committee is going to award Falconer his permission, while refusing to take the matter of a preservation order seriously?'

'It does look like it. I'm sorry, Ms Jordan.'

Alice headed back to her stall. That wretched man and his weasel words. He wasn't in the least sorry. She was almost back when she spotted Dominic and Chris Bryant, heads together, deep in conversation. Huh! Doubtless reporting on the discussion he'd just had with Alice.

To distract herself from the disturbing and very real probability that she had absolutely no chance of halting the construction of the leisure centre, she began counting the badges that were left. Zoe had managed to get rid of a few in Alice's absence, but nowhere near enough to make a real difference to the situation. Alice's shoulders slumped. By the end of the afternoon she'd shifted a few more, but the grand total was depressing.

She wrote another blistering article for the *Post* but Neil refused to print it. Even Zoe, after her first spirited show of support, was beginning to waver. 'I have to support Richard, Alice. I see that now. He's convinced they'll get the work and to be honest, the firm desperately needs it.'

'So suddenly the destruction of a historic woodland isn't so important.'

Zoe's face portrayed her distress.

'I'm sorry, Zoe,' Alice relented. 'I do understand. You have your family's well-being to consider.' That pronouncement didn't help, however. She was on her own; that was becoming increasingly evident.

★   ★   ★

Next morning an invitation arrived for Alice at the office. She was invited to a barbecue at Chelmleigh Manor at 8pm on July 23. *Dress casual.*

'Are you going?' she asked Neil.

'Wouldn't miss it. Do you want to go with me?'

Alice had been sorely tempted to bin the invitation, but had second thoughts. A high proportion of the townsfolk would most likely be there, and that would afford her another opportunity to canvass their support. In her enthusiasm, it didn't occur to her that Dominic might object to that.

Sadly, the extended period of good weather that they'd been enjoying broke on the morning of the 23rd. *Ha!* thought Alice, *the gods have decided to rain on his parade — or rather, his barbecue. Serves him right.*

However, by the time the evening came, the rain had stopped. Alice and Neil were making up a foursome with Zoe and Richard, so they walked to the manor house together. Dominic and

Belinda were waiting in front of the house to greet their guests. Belinda was dressed to the nines, Alice saw, in a low-cut blouse and perfectly tailored silk trousers, despite the invitation stipulating casual wear. 'I'd love to see her when she's really dressed up,' Alice muttered into Zoe's ear, 'if that's her idea of casual.'

'Look at Richard!' Zoe murmured back, 'His eyes have practically left his skull.' She nudged him. 'Stop gaping, darling. It's undignified.' She giggled.

She knew she had no need to worry. Richard adored her.

But Alice, darting a sideways glance at Neil, saw that if she did indeed have any serious intentions about him, then she *did* have cause to worry. He looked as gobsmacked as Richard, the difference being that he seemed to have the resolve to do something about it. He made a start by bending low over Belinda's hand, to brush his lips over the elegant, bejewelled fingers.

'I'm Neil Radcliffe, editor of the *Post*.'

'Oh.' Belinda snatched her hand away. 'Isn't it your paper that's running the campaign against Dominic?'

'Not really.' Neil's smile looked slightly strained. 'We have to give both sides of any argument or dispute. I do try to maintain a fair balance.'

'It's a pity your staff don't try to do the same then.' She shot a venomous glance at the unabashed Alice.

'Oh, I think they do — apart from the odd exception, and sometimes they have to be reined in,' Neil told her, taking care not to look at Alice.

The foursome moved on to skirt the house and reach the barbecue in the main garden at the rear. Alice was seething at what she saw as Neil's treachery. He should have defended her stance, said that all of his reporters enjoyed the freedom — more or less — to vent their own opinions. And how on earth could he be attracted to someone so — so *superficial?* And the sister-in-law to Dominic Falconer, her sworn enemy? She'd thought better of

Neil, but he was just like every other man, salivating over the sight of a cleavage, no matter who sported it.

'Wow!' exclaimed Zoe, completely oblivious to her friend's fury. 'Now that is what I call a barbecue.'

Alice sniffed disparagingly. Not for Dominic an ordinary gas-fuelled device: there stood a massive brick construction that could easily have roasted an ox or two and still had space left over. As it was two whole pigs were rotating side by side, filling the air with the mouthwatering aroma of crisply roasted pork. Beside this, under a large awning, there was a long table bearing a vast assortment of salads, bowls of cooked prawns, half a dozen sides of salmon, a huge slab of roast beef, plus more varieties of bread than Alice had ever seen before and enough cheeses to fill the average delicatessen counter.

A marquee had been set up on the lawn, presumably in case the rain returned. Glancing in, she discovered forty or so tables, each laid for twelve people with crisp white cloths and napkins, silver cutlery and wine glasses. As if that weren't enough, each table also bore a fat white candle set amongst an arrangement of summer blooms, along with bottles of red and white wine and a beautifully arranged bowl of fruit.

'He doesn't believe in skimping, does he?' Zoe murmured excitedly. 'There's even a dance floor. It must have cost him a packet.'

'Money well spent, he presumably thinks,' Alice said bitterly, 'if it keeps the entire town in his back pocket.'

'Oh, Alice,' Zoe chastised.

'Well, it looks as if the better part of the populace is here,' Alice observed, looking around at all the familiar faces flocking in. 'Who's going to speak out against him after this?'

Zoe dug her elbow into her friend's ribs. 'Keep your voice down,' she hissed. 'He's just over there.'

'Should I care?' Alice returned spiritedly.

'I was wondering — are they an item?'

'Who?' Alice paused.

'Dominic and the gorgeous Belinda, of course.'

'How should I know? I wouldn't think so. She is his sister-in-law.'

'Mmm, and widowed, I heard. So, who knows, hmm?'

Alice shrugged. If they were, they should suit each other admirably. 'Where's Neil?' She glanced around. He'd been with them a second ago.

'Dunno. Gone back to drool over the said sister-in-law, perhaps. She's nowhere to be seen, either.'

Once the guests had eaten their fill, to the accompaniment of a single harpist, and darkness had fallen, a rock band began to play. As it did so, a flash of lightning illuminated the night sky and a loud peal of thunder rumbled immediately overhead.

'Come on, Alice,' Neil coaxed. 'Let's dance and ignore the storm.' He'd appeared again after the other three had seated themselves at a table. He made no mention of where he'd been but, as

Belinda also walked in seconds afterwards, Alice presumed they'd been together.

The notion disturbed Alice. She'd always counted on knowing Neil was there, in the background so to speak, ready to do whatever she wanted of him. Selfish of her, maybe, but comforting, nonetheless. It looked as if that were about to change.

* * *

An hour later, Neil had disappeared once more and Richard and Zoe had wandered off to chat to some other friends, so Alice was sitting alone, staring into her half-empty glass of wine. Dejectedly, she topped it up from one of the bottles that still held some wine. Maybe she ought to start chatting to people, as she'd planned. After all, that was the reason for her presence here. But somehow, she didn't feel in the mood. The thunder was at last fading into the distance, leaving just the rain drumming loudly on the canvas of the marquee. She looked up at the roof. Miraculously, there were no leaks. She found herself half hoping there would be. Anything to mar the maddening perfection that Dominic had achieved; seemed to achieve in whatever he set out to do, if the stories she'd heard about him were true. She was thrusting the uncharitable thoughts to one side when she brought her glance back down — only to find Dominic standing in front of her. Surely, her thoughts couldn't have summoned him? Not even he was a mind-reader. Or was he? There didn't seem very much he wasn't capable of.

'Will you dance with me?' he asked.

Alice stared at him, open-mouthed. He'd been ignoring her all evening, she'd decided, watching him doing the rounds of his guests. Playing the perfect host, it seemed, to everyone bar her.

'Good heavens, lost for words? That must be a first.'

Alice pulled herself together. 'Not for

long,' she riposted.

Dominic grinned. 'Thought not.' He held out a hand and Alice found herself standing to take it. Against all of her expectations, she found the idea of being held by Dominic appealing. Thoroughly disconcerted by this surprising turn of events, she glanced around self-consciously, only to discover every eye upon her. She swallowed. Good grief. If she danced with him, would it be interpreted by everyone as conceding defeat? That was the last thing she wanted.

Dominic had started to laugh. 'Oh, Alice. You have such a delightfully expressive face. You'd never make a poker player.'

'Just as well I don't want to be one, then,' she retorted. 'I've got better things to do with my time — '

'Oh, I'm sure you have, but just for now, dance with me.' Without another word, he yanked her straight into his arms. 'Forget the battle against the evil developer and your attempt to get Chris Bryant to use his influence to secure that preservation order you've been after — '

'Ha! That's rich. If we're talking about trying to influence people . . . ' she blurted as they started to move in time to the music. Why had the band suddenly begun to play something smooth and smoochy? Up until now, they'd been banging out the rock covers. She glared at Dominic, but something in his gaze stopped her from going any further. Suddenly, she was positive that Chris Bryant had told him of his conversation with Alice on the afternoon of the fete. 'I merely asked him about the chances of getting it,' she lamely finished. 'By the way, where is the honourable member for Chelmleigh? I fully expected to see him here, as the pair of you are so obviously in cahoots.'

Dominic's eyes again hardened until they reminded her of tempered steel. 'If by 'in cahoots' you mean he wants the leisure centre built as much as the rest of Chelmleigh do, then you're absolutely correct. But he couldn't make it.

He had to get to Westminster. An important vote.'

'I thought they indulged in the convenient practice of pairing?'

'It wasn't practical.'

'Of course, it could be that he simply didn't want to be at your party.'

'Ouch! What sharp little claws you have.'

Just then, she saw what she'd been half-expecting all evening, right from the moment she'd seen Neil gazing, open-mouthed, at Belinda. The two of them were dancing so closely, they could have been Superglued together. Tears of frustration and yes, jealousy, stung Alice's long-lashed green eyes. How could he?

'Do you think you could try and relax a little, Alice?' Dominic murmured. 'It's like trying to dance with a gate post.'

Alice was incensed, and quite unexpectedly hurt. 'I've been called many things in my time,' she snapped, 'but gate post, I have to say, has not been one of them.'

'I'm not a big, bad wolf come to gobble you up.'

'That's debatable,' she muttered beneath her breath.

He heard her, of course, and she watched as that infernal eyebrow lifted and a smile that totally belied his last statement twisted his mouth. 'Of course, that's not to say that I wouldn't like to try.'

Alice's head jerked upwards as she stiffened in his grasp. Had she heard that correctly?

'You're doing it again — stiffening up.'

Well, what on earth did he expect her to do after a remark like that?

'Are you always this uptight when a man's holding you?' And he pulled her back in to him, so roughly that her chest bumped against his.

Alice gasped. 'That hurt.' He was as hard as iron. Was his chest made of steel, as well as his eyes?

'Sorry.' He clearly didn't mean it. 'You haven't answered my question.'

'And I don't intend to. It's none of your business what I do when a man's holding me.'

'Shame.' He gave a theatrical sigh. His eyes were dancing with amusement.

Alice had had enough. 'I think we've finished our dance.'

'We've hardly begun.' He looked genuinely startled at that, but he made no move to loosen his grip, and other than indulging in an undignified struggle to free herself, Alice was stuck where she was.

'Will you please let me go?' She spoke between clenched teeth. Surely he wouldn't ignore a direct appeal?

'I don't think so,' he drawled. 'I'm rather enjoying this.'

'Let me go!' she demanded. 'Now.'

'Why do you dislike me so?'

Alice opened her eyes wide at him. Could he really be that obtuse?

'Why on earth do you think?'

'Well, I know we disagree on my plans but surely we could still manage to be friends.'

'*Friends?*' she cried. 'I could never consider someone who is hell-bent on destruction a friend.'

'Why don't you admit you've lost this particular battle? You're outnumbered and outgunned. There's no shame in conceding defeat. You've tried your best.'

It was the last straw for Alice. 'I've not lost! Not yet. I will do everything in my power to stop you. I don't care what it takes. Are you listening?'

He was gazing into the far distance, but now, he snapped his attention back to her. 'Yes, I'm listening. How could I not be? Your mouth's only inches from my ear. I'm just considering how best to break the news to you.'

Alice felt a sinking feeling begin in the depths of her stomach. So over-whelming, that she could barely bring herself to ask, 'Break what news?'

'That I've got the planning permission I need. I received the letter this morning. We begin felling trees next week.'

6

Alice spent a totally sleepless night. Her mind was whirling with thoughts; plans; some so outrageous that even she knew they would be impossible to carry through. By the time morning came, however, she knew what she was going to do. All she needed was Neil's agreement — although if what she'd seen at the barbecue was anything to go by, he could well be totally on the Falconers' side by now.

He and Belinda had danced together for what remained of the evening, which hadn't been that long. Alice storming away from Dominic, leaving him standing alone in the middle of the dance floor, had effectively brought the evening to a close. People had started to drift away. Alice, Zoe and Richard had followed suit. Of Neil, there was no sign.

Alice had told Zoe what Dominic had said.

'Oh, Alice, I'm sorry.' Her friend put an arm around her.

'Well, I'm not,' Richard had chipped in. 'Maybe now we'll know who's got the building contract. I'm very optimistic that it will be us. So, Zoe, I'd appreciate it if you stay out of any further controversial behaviour.'

Arriving at work the following morning, Alice went straight in to see Neil.

'Hi, Neil, can I have a word?'

Neil looked at her, his face flushing. 'Alice, if it's about last night — '

'It isn't. Well, not directly.'

He'd clearly been going to apologise about deserting her for Belinda, but Alice wasn't interested in that. Not right now.

'Presumably you know that Dominic Falconer got his planning consent?'

'Yes. Um, Belinda told me.' He still looked uncomfortable.

'Naturally,' she said smoothly. 'I take it you were going to say something to me, in the event that Dominic didn't?'

'Yes . . . of course . . . '

'Well, I've spent the night forming my next course of action.'

Neil groaned. 'Alice, you've lost. There's nothing more you can do. It's going ahead.'

'Not if you agree to what I'm about to ask you. There's a chance still that he can be stopped.'

'Go on, then. What?'

'I want to organise a sit-in. Well, a sit-up really.'

'What on earth are you on about?'

'A sit-up — in the trees that are going to be felled. If I can get enough support, enough people occupying enough trees, they can't be chopped down. At least, not the ones we're sitting in.'

'We? And who's we?' Neil asked, leaning forward a trifle impatiently.

'Whoever I can persuade to do it.'

'For God's sake! Nobody will do it. When will you admit that? It's crazy.'

'No, it's not.' Her face was alight

with determination. 'I'm sure I can persuade — '

'In your dreams.'

'Give me twenty-four hours. I know I can get support. If I do, will you give me some time off? Consider me away on an investigative assignment?'

'For how long?' Neil looked astonished but, nevertheless, intrigued.

'For as long as it takes.'

'All right.' He gave a weary sigh. 'You're wasting your time, though.'

But Alice had already gone. She didn't have much time and, somehow, she had to drum up support. She couldn't do this on her own.

By that evening, however, she acknowledged it was going to be a great deal harder than she had supposed. The most frequent response to her request was, 'You're nuts. You're also wasting your time. The town needs a facility like the leisure centre.'

At the end of it all, no-one was prepared to help her. She realised, belatedly, that Neil had expected this. It was why he'd agreed so readily to her request for time off. He'd known it would only amount to one day.

She phoned him from the flat.

'So, how many people have agreed?' he asked.

'None. But I'm doing it anyway.'

'What? Alone?'

'Yeah. It's a great story. *Lone woman stops trees being chopped down.*'

'Dream on. Just you sitting in one tree won't stop it.'

'You want to bet? It would be too dangerous. Especially if I move around; if they can't tell exactly where I am.'

Neil didn't say anything.

'So can I still have the time off? I'll write a daily diary. I'd still be working. I could be an environmental Bridget Jones.'

To her astonishment, Neil agreed.

* * *

Alice wasted no time. It was essential that she positioned herself in the branches of a tree. She chose one, smack in the middle of the wood; a huge, spreading oak. It was the ideal place, its branches providing as secure a platform as any tree could.

Making herself as comfortable as possible, her back against the trunk, she made two phone calls on her mobile to fellow journalists, each of whom wrote for one of the national dailies. She was confident they'd write her story, thus giving her maximum publicity. She'd show Dominic Falconer that things weren't about to go as smoothly as he hoped. It might even generate the sort of help she so desperately needed. For Neil was right, of course. She couldn't prevent the felling indefinitely; not on her own. They'd simply get on with the work around her. All she could hope for was that her presence would delay things for a while.

However, not even Alice could have envisaged the strength of response that her story would generate. Just as she'd hoped, both nationals published her story and on the third day of her sit-up, Mrs Cooper arrived. She'd read the article in one of the papers and had hastened along to try and persuade Alice to abandon her campaign. Of Dominic Falconer or his henchmen, there had been no sign.

Alice, it had to be said, was weakening — fractionally. It had rained intermittently and despite the waterproofs she had had the forethought to bring along, she was feeling extremely wet and cold. In fact, she was beginning to feel she'd gladly trade her soul for a hot bath and a meal. So, when the old lady held up a flask of hot soup, Alice grabbed it gratefully.

'Alice, dear, this is madness. You'll end up with pneumonia or something. Please come down.'

It took a great deal of fortitude for Alice to say, 'No. I can't let them destroy this.' She waved her free hand around at the majestic trees.

'But you can't stop them. Not alone.'

She stopped talking abruptly. The

sounds of men's voices reached them.

'Alice — please!' she begged urgently. 'Come down, now. They're here. Please — Oh, dear me — '

Alice felt her heart thud as she peered through the dense greenery, straining to see how many men there were.

'Blimey, it's wet,' she heard someone exclaim. 'You have to hand it to her, sitting it out in this, alone.'

She heard the sounds of feet trampling the undergrowth, then, 'Can we get the van through?'

'Yeah, no problem. But let's find her first.'

The voices got louder. They were getting nearer. Alice braced herself for the sight of men with chainsaws. She heard Mrs Cooper groan, 'Oh no.'

So it was with great relief that Alice saw two youngish men and a slightly built, dark-haired girl, with no signs of a chainsaw between them, tramp out of the bushes. The tallest of the men hailed her.

'There you are! The lone warrior herself.' They all stood beneath the oak tree, the one who'd spoken holding out a hand to a stunned Mrs Cooper. 'Hi, I'm Crusoe.' He pointed to the shorter man. 'This is Star and that's Eden. We've come to help. The rest of the team will be here tomorrow.'

★   ★   ★

Sure enough, a small army of people arrived the following morning, after which it took just three days to erect a virtual encampment of tree houses. Crusoe and Star worked unceasingly — as did Alice and most of the other protesters.

She now had reasonably comfortable accommodation: a stout wooden platform with a canvas sheet to provide shelter from the elements. A rope ladder gave easy access. There were even the rudimentary beginnings of what looked like rope bridges spanning the gaps between a few of the more substantial and important, centrally-positioned trees. Crusoe had told her that this was so that some protesters could always remain aloft, a fact of vital importance in times of crisis. If there were protesters in the trees, who couldn't be removed, then they couldn't be felled. And as they were positioned smack in the middle of the endangered wood, it made clearing the entire area a virtual impossibility. Alice realised with more than a twinge of alarm that they were preparing for full-scale war.

'So, whaddya think?' It was Star. Alice swung round to look at him. He didn't present a very prepossessing picture, with his almost emaciated face and body, lank hair and the piercings that adorned almost every visible part of his anatomy. Despite this, Alice had grown to like him, as she did Crusoe. Crusoe was fractionally more conventional in appearance, with tidier hair and just one earring. He was also more substantially built.

Eden, Alice supposed, was his girl-friend, although no-one had actually told her that. Eden certainly behaved as if they were. But Alice wasn't sure that Crusoe viewed her in the same light. He behaved much more casually towards her, at times almost rebuffing her if she got too close. In fact, Alice thought she'd glimpsed a glitter of desire in his eyes whenever he looked at her — Alice. She wasn't unhappy about that. Crusoe was an attractive man, with his flaxen hair and startlingly blue eyes, a nose that was pure Grecian and a mouth to die for. Full-lipped and cleanly chiselled, when he smiled it revealed a set of perfect teeth. All in all, she wouldn't be at all averse to a spot of flirtation. Mind you, what Eden would think of that, she wasn't sure.

'I think you've done this many times before,' she remarked to Star.

'A couple. That's how I met Crusoe. It was his decision to come and help you. He's the boss of the group.' Star's green eyes shone at her. They were his most striking characteristic, along with the distinctive jacket he always wore. It was made of faded blue denim and had a huge, cut-out silk eagle stitched onto the back.

Alice glanced round now, rather uncertainly. More vans and caravans had arrived and were parked indiscriminately along the perimeter of the wood — along with the sort of rubbish and litter that were the inevitable result of normal, daily living. There were even lines of washing hung out to dry. It was a mess. Alice frowned. This wasn't what she had envisaged. Her gaze moved on. 'What are Crusoe and Eden doing?'

'Hammering bolts into the trunks of trees. They'll break the chainsaws when they hit them.'

'But won't they damage the trees?' Alice asked doubtfully.

'You mean, more than the chainsaws will? Chill. Crusoe knows exactly what he's doing.'

Alice hoped he did. He and several others were now wrapping barbed wire around the trunks, Crusoe's muscles rippling with the effort. She wondered what his real name was? He looked up suddenly and caught her staring. He grinned, and Alice felt her heart lurch.

'Is Crusoe his real name?'

'Nah. His name's Robinson Latimer. He hates it. So he calls himself Crusoe. Robinson Crusoe — see?'

'Yes. of course.'

'He's brilliant. Trained as a doctor, but decided to drop out when he realised he'd probably spend all his time trying to compensate for the deficiencies of the NHS. His words, not mine.'

'How old is he?'

'Twenty-seven, eight; not really sure. Age doesn't come into it, really.'

'No.' She paused. Was she being too nosy? As Star didn't seem to mind her questions, she asked, 'And why are you called Star?'

'Short for Stargazer. I study the stars.'

The next day, the banners went up.

Huge white sheets daubed with the words SAVE OUR WOODS and HANDS OFF OUR TREES were suspended along the perimeter of the wood, in clear view of the road. The group were incredibly well-organised. She couldn't have done all this on her own. There was even someone whose sole duty it was to feed the protesters. Where this food was coming from, Alice didn't enquire.

Crusoe, to her delight, was spending a fair amount of time with her. They discussed everything and anything; no subject was taboo. He was a highly intelligent man, she discovered.

'Do you regret giving up the medical profession?' she asked him.

'Oh ho, someone been talking?'

'Sorry, my fault. I asked Star.' She blushed beneath his twinkling gaze. She hadn't meant to let him know that she'd been asking about him.

'I don't mind. In fact, I'm flattered that you were interested enough to ask.' he gave her a long, intense look.

Alice broke out in a sweat. Ooh, he was gorgeous!

'So, in answer to your question, no, I don't regret a thing. If I hadn't given it up, I wouldn't have met you.'

Alice thought she was about to explode into flame, then, beneath that smouldering, passionate gaze.

'Anyway, enough of that — ' he gave a slow smile, a smile full of promise — 'for now. Instead, why don't you fill me in on this Dominic Falconer?'

7

Alice was trying to tidy her living quarters the next day when she heard someone climbing up her rope ladder. Her heart leapt. Was it Crusoe? She hoped so.

But it wasn't the man who'd seemed to be invading her thoughts at all sorts of odd moments. It was Eden.

'Hi,' the girl said. 'You look disappointed. Expecting someone else?'

'Um — no, not really. What can I do for you?'

'Lay off Crusoe.' Deep brown eyes lasered Alice, as the slightly too large mouth tightened. Eden raked long fingers through her dishevelled chestnut hair. She wasn't unattractive, Alice decided, but there was a very hard look to her. As if she were used to getting her own way.

''Lay off'?' Alice was speechless.

'Pardon me, but who are you to tell me what to do? Or Crusoe, come to that? He's a free agent, isn't he?'

'No. Not any more. He's with me, and has been for some time.'

'Oh, really? He doesn't seem to see it that way. And it's certainly not the impression I've received.'

'Oh, I'm sure it isn't. But let's face it, *Alice*,' she emphasised the name, 'any man will make a move, won't he, when he sees the green light blazing.'

'Green light?' Alice smiled. 'We aren't talking traffic signals here.'

'Oh, come on. You've barely taken your eyes off him since we arrived. What's up? Can't get a man of your own, so you decide to pinch mine?'

'I think you'd better discuss this with Crusoe.'

'Oh, believe me, I will. I just thought I'd warn you first.'

'Right, well, you've done that, so now you can leave.'

As Eden began to descend the ladder, Alice saw a strange expression appear on her face.

'Just watch your back, Alice.'

Alice's eyes widened. 'Are you threatening me?'

'Make of it what you will.' Eden sang, 'Byee,' waved, and was gone.

★ ★ ★

That afternoon it was Star who called up to Alice. 'Someone's turned up to see you.'

'Is it important? I'm working.' She'd been trying to drag her thoughts away from Eden's words, and the suspicion that they'd presented some kind of threat, by working on the daily diary that she'd promised to write for the paper. Now that there was a crowd of protesters to safeguard the wood, she could take time out and go to the office to transfer her written notes onto her computer there.

'He says it is. It's Dominic Falconer.'

She'd been expecting this. In fact, she was surprised it had taken this long.

Carefully, she put down the notebook she'd been writing in and stood up. She'd go down and face him on his own level, no matter how tempted she was to stay put in the tree and merely shout down to him.

She'd barely set foot on the ground before he challenged, 'Have you seen what your . . . *friends* are doing to this place?'

'Nice to see you, too,' she replied. Really, did he have to be so rude? Whatever had happened to *good day, how are you?* Although, she should have expected this, she supposed. He didn't respond, other than to raise that maddening eyebrow at her. 'Of course I've seen.'

'Doesn't it bother you?' he cut in. 'This so-called 'saving' of the wood?' His tone was pure scorn. 'After all the fuss you've been making, you're doing as much damage as a chainsaw.'

'How do you work that out? You'd chop the trees down, every last one. All we've done is erect a few tree houses — '

'As well as create several dozen piles of festering rubbish. And then there are the hordes of people trampling and destroying the very undergrowth you're so keen on preserving. What value nature's balance now, eh?' he asked sarcastically. 'I did actually intend retaining a lot of the trees, incorporating them into the design. The way you're going on, there won't be anything left to retain. And that's not to mention the squirrels. Seen anything of them lately, by the way?'

'Alice, everything okay? I'm Crusoe, by the way. Who are you?' Crusoe slid an arm about Alice's waist, possessively, protectively. Dominic's gaze narrowed as he stared down at it contemptuously.

'I'm Dominic Falconer, the man who wants you off his land. But I can see how things stand.' And again his glance went to Crusoe's arm.

'You don't see anything,' Alice shouted furiously at him. 'What have you come here for?'

'I came as a matter of courtesy to

inform you that I've applied for an eviction order against you and your friends.' His top lip curled. 'To give you the opportunity to leave the area peacefully and without trouble. As probably your precious squirrels have already done.'

'A lot of good an eviction order will do you,' she said contemptuously.

Slate eyes glinted at her from beneath lowered lids, as he softly said, 'I think it will do me very well. You see,' he leaned towards her, his breath feathering her face, his aftershave filling her nostrils, 'I'm going to get you off this land, you and your cohorts — you have my word on that. It's just a matter of days so, if I were you, I'd start packing — now.'

★   ★   ★

As if that announcement weren't bad enough, Neil showed up at the wood an hour later and what he had to say left Alice practically spitting nails.

'I've just had Falconer on the phone.

He's applied for an eviction order.'

'I know,' Alice snapped. 'Just let him try and evict us.'

'Alice, Alice, you can't win this battle.' His gaze went to Crusoe, who had stayed at Alice's side. 'He said you seem to have made a friend — '

'I've made lots of friends, Neil.'

'A *special friend*, he told me.' It was slyly said, with a meaningful glance at Crusoe. It was only too evident what he was implying. That she and Crusoe were in a relationship.

Alice was outraged, even though she'd had the same thoughts — well, wishes, really — herself. And it certainly wouldn't be beyond the realms of possibility. '*What?*'

'You know very well.'

'Crusoe, can you leave us?' Alice said, endeavouring to keep her temper. Crusoe was grinning broadly by this time, adding to her embarrassment.

'Are you sure, now?' Crusoe altered his expression to one of exaggerated concern.

'Yes,' Alice once more snapped. He was enjoying this. Just as Neil was. Men! She hated them all at that moment.

Once Crusoe had gone, Alice faced Neil. 'I don't know what exactly Dominic said to you, but — '

'Why, that you and — Crusoe, isn't it? — have got something going. You know, a romance. It would make a great story. *Love blossoms in the midst of battle.*' He spread his hands as if showing her the headline. 'Can I have a photograph of you together?'

'No, you flippin' well can't. There's nothing like that going on.'

'Oh, shame. Couldn't you maybe get something going, then?'

'Neil! Just go. I'll bring my diary to the office in a day or two.'

She sought out Crusoe the minute Neil had left. She wanted to warn him about the things Dominic had told Neil, just in case the story should be printed. She realised she didn't quite trust Neil any more — and supposing

Eden read it? What then? Would she carry out what had sounded dangerously like a threat? Would Alice disappear, never to be seen again? She shook herself. What nonsense. What could Eden do to her?

To her relief, all Crusoe did was laugh. 'Chill, Alice. I'm not bothered.'

No, thought Alice, *but your self-styled girlfriend might be.*

'But you heard what Falconer said. He's getting an eviction order.'

'Best of luck to him. He'll find it impossible to get us out of a tunnel.'

'A tunnel?' So that's what all the noise had been. She hadn't realised, she'd been too busy drafting out her diary. And the work had been on the other side of the wood. They could have been digging miles of it and she wouldn't have been any the wiser.

'Yeah. Large enough to take most of the people here. Once we're inside, they'll find it almost impossible to evict us.'

But, for all her desire to save the

trees, Alice was feeling increasingly concerned about the way things were going. When she'd planned her protest, she hadn't envisaged so much — well, Dominic was right to a certain degree — *damage* being done in the process. And he was right about something else, too. She'd seen no sign of any red squirrels; the whole point of her protest in the first place. She knew they were shy, but still . . .

Her unhappy glance swept over the barbed wire-wrapped trees, the heaps of rotting rubbish, and now — what would be the effects of a tunnel being dug? What would that do to the roots of the very trees she was fighting to preserve? Her gaze roamed the banners, starting to look tatty and torn. Then she saw a movement, in the shadows beneath the trees on the edge of the woodland.

It was a man. He was just standing there, watching silently. He obviously didn't want to be recognised, because he was attired in a long, dark coat and some sort of wide-brimmed hat. A disguise? She stared harder. It wasn't Dominic; he wasn't tall enough — or bulky enough. In any case, he wouldn't stand in the shadows. It wasn't his way; he'd come straight out and confront her. She frowned. There was something familiar about him, though; especially the way in which he held himself.

Why, it was Sam, Richard's brother! Suddenly she was sure.

What was he doing? Was he spying? For Richard? But why? Why wouldn't Richard come along himself and see what was happening? She knew Richard was keen for them all to be gone, so that work could begin. She was about to go over and ask him that, when it was as if he sensed her intention, because he whirled about and was gone.

So, she mused, he definitely didn't want to talk to anyone, or have them know it was him, which again suggested a furtive aspect to the whole thing.

★ ★ ★

Days later, they received news that two houses had been burgled on a nearby housing estate.

'The word is,' they were told by a protester who had walked into town to buy supplies, 'that it's one of us.'

'What was stolen?' Alice asked.

'Money and jewellery. A piece of the jewellery turned up in a second-hand shop in Chelmleigh. Not very bright. To steal it here and then immediately fence it here. Any of us would have more sense.'

Which did seem to suggest to Alice that it wouldn't be beyond the realms of possibility for one or two of the camp's residents to resort to theft to supply themselves with the wherewithal to live. And not just to live. More than once in the past days, Alice had detected the distinctive odour of cannabis. And for that, they needed funds.

Nobody was surprised when two policemen turned up later that day. Crusoe had questioned everyone in the camp and told Alice that he believed their denials of any involvement in the crimes. 'I've known these guys for some time now and they wouldn't go out thieving. No way.' So Alice intended telling the police that, in no uncertain terms. After all; she was known in the local community because of her news reporting, so surely they would take her word for the protesters' innocence?

She was swiftly disabused of that notion.

'You have a young man here who wears a jacket with an eagle sewn onto the back, I believe?' one officer asked her self-importantly once she had introduced herself.

'Yes,' Alice answered. 'He's called Star.'

'Right. So how do you explain the fact that Star was seen running from one of the houses which was burgled?'

'Well, I can't — obviously,' Alice said less confidently.

'Quite.' The policeman smiled smugly. 'We'd like to question him in that case, in connection with both burglaries.'

'Star wouldn't do anything like that,' Alice protested.

'Nonetheless, we'd still like to question him.'

'As far as I know, Star hasn't left the camp site.'

'You're sure of that are you, Ms Jordan?'

'Well, no, but — What day and what time did these burglaries take place?'

'At midday, yesterday and the day before, when both houses were empty. The occupants all being at work.'

'I'm sure Star was here then.'

'In which case, he should be able to answer our questions satisfactorily. We just need someone to have definitely seen him at those times.'

'Who saw him leaving the house?'

The policeman flicked open his notebook. 'A John Davis. But it was a Mr Sam Willis who, upon hearing a description of what the burglar was wearing, came to us and reported having seen a young man here, in the camp, wearing a similar jacket.'

Of course. Sam. He'd been at the camp, where he'd obviously spotted Star and his jacket.

Alice didn't know what to think then. She would have staked her life on Star's honesty. But if he'd been seen, running from the scene of the crime — ? And his jacket was very distinctive. But would he really have been that stupid? To wear it to commit a crime?

*　*　*

Eventually, a white-faced Star rejoined them. Several of the protesters had said that they'd seen him in the camp at the crucial times. 'They had to let me go,' he said.

Despite this, Alice remained uneasy. Star had been positively identified. So had the protesters lied about his where-abouts at the times of the burglaries? Or did someone else have a similar jacket? Either way, she could foresee trouble.

It didn't take long for her fears to be

realised. A crowd of townsfolk duly turned up, some adults, but mainly youths, residents of the estate that had been burgled. They began shouting. 'Clear off! We don't need the likes of you. Thieves, scum, liars. Protecting one of your own, eh? We know it was him. He was seen.'

Stones began to be hurled. One of the protesters was struck on the cheek. Alice started forward. The adults would know who she was. She thought she recognised a couple. She'd talk to them, try to reassure them.

'Where's our jewellery?' one of them demanded of Alice.

'Yeah, and our money?' another said. 'That was for our holiday.'

Several more stones flew through the air. This time, one struck Alice. She lifted a hand to her forehead and brought it away covered in blood.

'And *you*,' one of the men shouted, pointing his finger straight at Alice. 'Traitor. Bringing these sort of people into our town. Why don't you leave with them when they go?'

It was the signal for a veritable hail of sticks and stones to rain down on the protesters, forcing them back into the shelter of the trees, before suddenly, it was all over. People began backing away, as if realising they'd gone too far. Either that, or they'd seen the powerful car speeding towards the woodland.

'Oh no,' groaned Alice, her hand clasped to her head. Could things get any worse? It was Dominic. Surely he hadn't put people up to this? Although, it would suit his purposes, to have the protesters driven away.

He brought the car to a sliding halt yards from where Alice stood, and climbed out. His face seemed hewn from granite, so stony and set was it, and he was glowering at her. Alice didn't hesitate. She turned away and hastened back to the tree that she resided in. She'd had enough. Her head ached abominably and she couldn't face a further argument with him.

Swiftly she climbed the rope ladder,

convinced he would refuse to pursue her. Once on her platform, she looked down. The wretched man was standing there, looking up at her.

'What do you want?' she called down. Her head was still bleeding, the cut was evidently deeper than she'd believed. Groping in her jeans pocket, she found a relatively clean paper handkerchief and pressed it to the cut.

'What on earth have you done to yourself now?' he demanded.

'*I* haven't done anything. One of your followers heaved a stone at me.'

His jaw tightened even more. Now, it seemed chiselled from solid concrete. 'Whoever did that had nothing to do with me.'

'Well, you would say that, wouldn't you?' she called defiantly.

He stared up at her. 'Are you accusing me of inciting violence?'

Alice shrugged. She could hardly accuse him outright. Who knew what he would do?

'You are, aren't you?' His slate eyes turned almost black, and several tiny gold flecks appeared in them. 'You really do enjoy skating on thin ice, don't you, Alice? I warned you once before about making rash judgments about me.' She could see him fighting to maintain his cool, but he must have lost the battle because he growled, 'You really are the end. You've accused me of bribery and corruption, and now you imply that I'm inciting mob violence. What else are you going to accuse me of?'

'How about setting up a burglar to look like Star — ?' She stopped abruptly. Oh! Now she'd done it.

'What exactly do you mean by that?' His voice was low and menacing.

'Well, it wasn't Star who broke in and robbed those people, so s-someone must have made it look as if it was. Th-they copied his jacket design — ' She swallowed hard. He looked murderous. What if he climbed up and — and — ? 'Either that, or — or someone is lying.'

Dominic stayed where he was. She offered up a small prayer of thanks.

He stared at her long and hard, but declined to answer her ridiculous suggestion. 'What I came to tell you was that I've got the eviction order.'

'Huh! Chris Bryant been doing as he's told again? How much did . . . ' But something in his expression warned her to stop right there. She did.

'You've got four days to clear off. If you're all still here after that time, I'll forcibly evict you.'

'I think not. But do your worst.'

'Oh, believe me, I intend to. You haven't seen anything like my worst so far. If you want my advice, you'll go home and leave what's going to happen next to the battle-hardy.'

'By battle hardy, you mean — ?' she asked guilelessly.

'The riff-raff you've chosen to consort with. Thieves, villains, good-for-nothings. What do you think that makes you?' he demanded scathingly.

'What? You're calling me a thief?' she cried in horror.

He didn't immediately answer. 'If you consort with — '

''Consort'? 'Consort'?' she sarcastically echoed. 'For heaven's sake, get down off your high horse. I'll have you know I'm no more a thief than — than any of these people are. They're honest, genuine, caring — which is more than can be said of you. I'd stake my reputation on their good characters.'

He laughed, shortly. 'You might have to. I wouldn't think your editor would be keen to employ a reporter who could possibly be implicated in a series of burglaries.'

'A *series* of burglaries?' She mimicked his cynical laugh. 'Hardly that.'

'No? You obviously haven't heard, then.'

A sensation of foreboding engulfed Alice. ''Heard what?'

'There's been another break-in and, again, a man was seen running away from the house. A man wearing a jacket with an eagle stitched on its back. Ring any bells?'

Alice fell silent. Whoever the burglar was — and she was even more convinced now that it wasn't Star, as he wouldn't be stupid enough to do it again — he couldn't be very proficient. He'd been seen twice now.

Something struck her. Had he *intended* to be seen? Intended that Star should shoulder the blame? It would surely provoke even more violent behaviour from the local community. Was that the intention?

'Look,' Dominic went on, 'you're clearly not up to all of this. You've already managed to injure your-self — '

'I've already pointed out, I didn't injure myself. Your supporters did that.'

His glance softened as it rested upon her cut forehead, and a strange look appeared on his face. 'Alice, please — I don't want to see you hurt, really hurt. Please come down.'

Alice couldn't believe it. The great

Dominic Falconer was actually pleading with her. 'I'm not going anywhere.' Her defiance blazed out.

'Okay then, I'll come up there and get you.'

8

Alice couldn't believe what she was hearing. The super-rich property magnate, shinning up a rope ladder to get his hands on her? 'What?'

With a marked show of long-suffering patience, Dominic began to repeat, 'I'll come up and — '

'Yes, yes,' Alice exploded. 'I heard you.'

'Then why did you say what?'

'How dare you? Who do you think you are? Telling me what to do. You just try coming up here — '

But he was already climbing the rope ladder with an expertise that made it look as if he'd been doing it for years.

Alice could only stand and watch, before she realised he was getting nearer with every second that passed. She took a hasty step backwards. He couldn't be more than a couple of feet from the platform now. Frantic, she looked around for a weapon, any sort of weapon. She had to stop him reaching her. Her glance alighted upon a pile of books Mrs Cooper had brought for her. She grabbed a couple — they were substantial tomes and reasonably heavy.

Dominic's head appeared above the platform. 'Planning to do a spot of reading?' he drawled sarcastically. Knowing amusement blazed from his eyes. 'Do you think you have the time?' He smiled now, with maddening complacency.

'Don't you come near me!' she spat.

'I recall you saying that to me once before — on our first meeting. I ignored you then, too.'

He was hoisting himself onto the platform. Wildly, Alice looked around. The platform was perched halfway up the tree. Plenty of room to climb higher. Surely, he wouldn't follow her up there? She dropped the books, one landing on her toes. She winced. Nonetheless, it didn't stop her pushing aside the canvas that gave her shelter from the elements, leaping for the first substantial branch and heaving herself up onto it.

'Alice!' Dominic shouted. 'Don't be stupid. If you should fall — '

'I'll hold you responsible!' she yelled back, starting to climb. It wasn't easy. The trunk was slippery, it had rained in the night again, so she couldn't manage to get a really secure grip.

'For goodness' sake, let's talk about this. Come down, at once.'

It gave Alice great pleasure to look down on him and say, 'No.' She was several feet above his head by this time, well up in the main canopy of the tree. She was surrounded by verdant foliage, almost completely hidden from him. She half turned to grin triumphantly down at him — and that was her undoing. She missed her footing and to her horror, felt herself begin to slip downwards. She made a grab for the next branch but couldn't catch hold. She began to fall — well, slide, really. It felt like being on a helter skelter; she couldn't halt her descent. Her nails broke, branches slapped her in the face. 'Aaaagh!' she screamed. She was dropping faster, branches snapping all around her, leaves spinning like confetti. She heard Dominic shout, 'Grab a branch — anything. Oh, no — '

She sensed rather than saw him make a tremendous leap forward and the next thing she knew, he was catching her, breaking her fall. Her relief didn't last long, however. The wooden platform shook beneath them. She heard a crack, and then another — the wood was splintering. They were going to fall to the ground.

'Hold on,' Dominic grimly told her, 'we're going — '

But no. Crusoe and his mates had done their job well. The planking held, just, and she and Dominic both toppled backwards, Alice landing awkwardly and painfully upon one foot.

She yelled. 'My ankle. I've broken my ankle . . . '

Once they'd recovered their balance, Alice leaning heavily on Dominic, she said furiously, 'That was your fault. If you'd left me alone, none of this would never have happened, would it? Now, I've gone and broken my — '

'Oh, shut up, woman, do,' Dominic retaliated roughly. 'You haven't broken anything.'

'How do you know what I've done?' she demanded indignantly.

'If you'd broken it you'd be yelling a darn sight louder than you are now.'

Alice glared at him. He'd just told her to shut up. 'How dare you?'

But something about his pallor stopped her. 'Oh, don't tell me you're hurt too . . . '

He grimaced. 'Ever the compassion- ate one. No, Alice, I'm not hurt — just winded. You're not the lightest of women I've ever had dropping on me.

In fact, now I come to think of it, you're the only woman I've ever had drop on me.' A small smile quirked his lips and colour began to return to his face.

'Oh, thanks!' she sniffed. He'd just called her fat. The beast!

'At last, some gratitude.'

'That's not gratitude. I'm responding to your implication that I'm fat. It was a sarcastic riposte. And for your information, I weigh — '

'Oh, for goodness' sake.' He glanced down all of a sudden. The platform was once more creaking alarmingly. 'I think we'd better get down off this thing. I suspect the whole structure is about to collapse any second now. Come on, I'll help you.'

This time, Alice didn't argue, and with Dominic's assistance, she began to climb down gingerly. They reached the ground to discover Crusoe awaiting them.

'What happened? I heard you scream.'

'I fell,' Alice told him, 'thanks to Mr Falconer here.'

Dominic merely raised his eyebrows at this.

'Are you hurt?' Crusoe asked.

'Yes, my ankle.' The trauma of it all was starting to affect Alice. She felt decidedly shaky; sick, in fact. 'I'm — I'm — ' Her head was spinning. She swayed.

'Alice!' Dominic reached out for her, just as she sank slowly into unconsciousness.

She came to to find herself lying on the ground, both men bending over her. Dominic was the first to speak. 'You're coming with me. You need to see a doctor.'

'I'm a doctor,' Crusoe volunteered.

'Really!' Dominic was manifestly unimpressed. 'Strange place for a doctor to be practising.'

Alice struggled to sit up. 'I'm not going anywhere with you.'

'Yes, you are. Your head's been quite badly cut, which could explain the fainting, and that ankle needs checking out. I presume you don't have an X-ray

139

machine hidden in a bush anywhere, doctor?' This sarcastic request was directed at Crusoe. 'No? So you need a professional to have a look at your injuries, and as I suppose I'm at least partly responsible for your fall — '

'Ha! Don't you mean wholly responsible?'

'Quite. Which is why I'm not taking no for an answer.' She'd fallen neatly — stupidly — into his trap. 'It's my business, therefore, to get it put right.'

Alice had already opened her mouth, fully intending to reply to this assertion when, in a single smooth movement, he swept her into his arms.

'Put me down,' she commanded furiously.

'No.' Dominic started to walk towards his Range Rover.

'Will you put me down?' Alice was helpless with indignation. The arrogant, insufferable — ! 'Crusoe,' she decided to try another tack, 'tell him you can see to my ankle.'

Crusoe spread his arms. 'Sorry.

Nothing I can do.'

'Well, thanks a bunch,' Alice muttered. 'What price loyalty?'

'At least one of you has seen sense,' Dominic retorted drily. 'You may as well stay quiet because, believe me, you are going to see a doctor. I don't want you suing me for compensation a couple of months down the line.'

Alice smiled grimly. 'And there I was, thinking you were concerned about me. I should have known better.'

But Dominic was paying her no attention at all. They'd reached his vehicle and he was breathing rather heavily as he struggled to open the passenger door while still holding her in his arms.

Alice smirked. As he'd so insultingly implied moments ago, she was no size zero model. Served him right. He shouldn't have just carried her off.

The door swung open and he thrust her into the seat. 'Now, be quiet.'

'Ever the gentleman,' she retaliated. 'I can see, now, how you've managed to charm the entire population of Chelmleigh. Such is the effectiveness of your silver-edged tongue.'

'Which is more than can be said of yours,' he returned. He strode around to the driver's side of the car and climbed in.

'My doctor is Doctor Morton,' she informed him.

'Mine is Ruskin. You'll be seeing him.'

Alice didn't reply. She was feeling sick again.

Dominic looked at her in astonishment. 'My word. No argument?'

'What's the point?' Alice murmured in a small voice. All of a sudden, she was too exhausted to do or say anything. Her head ached abominably and her ankle was hurting.

Dominic reached out a hand. 'Alice — '

With a painful effort, Alice jerked away from him. She saw his jaw harden but he said nothing.

It took several moments of fast driving before Alice had cause to wonder where they were headed. She was positive that Doctor Ruskin's surgery was in the other direction to the one in which they were travelling. 'Where are we actually going?'

'To the manor, of course.' She noticed he didn't look at her as he spoke.

'The manor! I thought we were going to the doctor's — '

'He'll come to us.'

She should have known. Mind you, that wasn't really such a bad idea. She had closed her eyes and so didn't notice the curious way in which Dominic regarded her. There was an oddly tender expression upon his face.

'I think I'd rather go home, in that case.'

'I don't think so.'

Her eyes snapped open. 'Why not? The doctor can come to there just as easily, can't he?'

'I want to keep an eye on you. You've had a nasty fall, plus that head wound. You could have concussion, for all we know.'

She eyed him with deep suspicion at that. 'What do you mean, *keep an eye on me*? For how long?'

'Just a few days.'

'A few days?' she echoed in horror. 'No way! I'm not staying with you for an hour, let alone a few days. Why, I've got things to do — '

'Like what?' he asked calmly.

'Well, my job, for one thing. Neil's expecting a daily diary — '

'So? You can still do that. I own a computer, and we do have that modern contraption that they call a phone.'

'No! Definitely not.'

'Right. Fine.' He brought the vehicle to a screeching halt. Alice looked at him in amazement.

'What if there'd been someone behind you?'

He ignored her rebuke. 'Okay. Off you go, then.' He leaned across her to open her door.

'What — you mean — now? Walk home?' Alice was aghast.

'If that's what you want to do, I won't stop you.'

'You know I can't walk!' she yelled.

'Precisely.' He leaned over her once again, and this time closed the door. 'So, come with me and I'll take care of you.'

There was nothing she could say to that calm statement. Defeated, she did the only thing she could, she sank back into her seat and closed her eyes. She certainly couldn't bring herself to look at him.

Oh no. She sat bolt upright. Once local people heard she was staying with him, they'd assume she'd given up on her fight.

She squinted sideways at him, her brow pulled down in a frown. The action made her head ache again. 'Did you plan all of this?'

'All of what?' He regarded her with a puzzled look. 'Plan your fall? How on earth could I have done that?'

'Well, it does suit you, doesn't it? To have me at your mercy, in your house. I mean, what will people think?'

He shrugged. 'And who cares about what people think? I certainly don't.'

'I do,' she snarled.

He sighed. 'Alice, I didn't plan anything. Your fall was an accident.'

She eyed him. 'Hmmm.'

Moments later, they drove through the imposing gates of Chelmleigh Manor and along the sweeping, tree-lined driveway. Without a word, Dominic climbed out of the car and strode round to the passenger side. He opened the door and hauled Alice out into his arms.

'I can walk,' she protested.

'Okay.' He promptly put her down, none too gently.

'Ouch!' Alice shrieked. 'You — '

'See,' he said smugly, picking her up again. 'You can't even stand, let alone walk. There's nothing for it, you'll have to stay here.' They'd reached the front door by now. 'Can you push the bell, please? My hands are otherwise occupied.'

Alice glared at him. He wasn't even

breathing heavily, she noted. So much for his claims about her weight. They'd obviously been grossly exaggerated. In fact, she wouldn't be surprised if he hadn't deliberately made himself sound out of breath.

Alice, defiant to the last, simply crossed her arms over her chest. He'd abducted her against her will; let him manage now, without any assistance from her. It was childish, she knew, but she didn't care.

'Have it your own way,' was all he said, clearly not the least bit put out by her obstinacy. He slid his one arm further beneath her, lifting her slightly, and pressed the doorbell. However, what Alice hadn't bargained for was that the simple action would bring her face up to within an inch of his. She bit her bottom lip as their breaths mingled and his slate eyes met hers in barely concealed amusement. As before, tiny gold flecks appeared in their depths.

Alice felt her heart race and her

pulse rate double. Was he aware of what was happening to her? She suspected from the glint in his eye that he was.

To Alice's relief, the door opened almost at once. Belinda stood there. Fancy! She would have expected the housekeeper to undertake that duty, not the haughty Belinda.

'What on earth has happened?' She was clearly shocked to see Alice in Dominic's arms, and not too pleased at that. 'Why is *she* here? And why are you carrying her?'

Alice felt like the cat that was being dragged in, but Dominic didn't waste time replying. He was beginning to pant slightly. Alice smirked. Ha! Not quite so all-powerful, then? Brushing past his outraged sister-in-law, he went straight into a large, light room, where he deposited Alice onto an enormous, white leather settee.

'Dominic?' Belinda asked again.

'We had an accident,' he told her curtly.

'We had an accident?' Alice echoed ironically. 'I don't see very much wrong with you.'

'You mean apart from an aching back from having to heft you around?' He stood over her, glowering.

Alice fell silent. Did he have to keep banging on about her weight? All right, she wasn't the thinnest of women, but she was far from fat. A rather modest eight stone six pounds, her scales had read the last time she'd weighed herself. Which, considering her height of five feet five inches, was about right. He was still looking pale, she noticed. Had he injured himself? She had her mouth open to ask him when Belinda did it for her.

'Are you hurt, Dominic?'

'Just my wrist. I twisted it slightly trying to catch Al — Ms Jordan.'

Alice instantly felt a rush of guilt. 'Alice will do,' she said in a low voice. Although he'd been calling her 'Alice' for the past half hour, he'd suddenly reverted to 'Ms Jordan'.

Why? Could it have anything to do with Belinda?

He gave a mocking bow. 'Thank you. Well, Alice will be staying here.'

His gaze didn't leave Alice as he spoke.

'Staying here?' Belinda cried. 'Why? She looks perfectly all right to me.'

Alice was suddenly fed up with it all. She wanted desperately to be in her own flat and she certainly didn't want to stay where she wasn't wanted. She struggled to get up.

'Stay there,' Dominic commanded.

'No. I'm going home. I can see that Mrs Falconer agrees with me.'

'Oh.' He folded his arms across his chest and stood before her, legs apart, blocking her from moving in any way. 'And how do you propose getting there? Because I'm not driving you.'

Alice sank back, defeated for the second time by his inflexibility. As for Belinda, she turned and stalked from the room.

'I'm just causing trouble — '

'No, you're not.'

Alice didn't have sufficient energy left to argue.

9

The doctor arrived in under 15 minutes, much to Alice's vexation. Had he been somewhere, meekly awaiting Dominic's summons? It wouldn't surprise her. Dominic Falconer was a man who would demand instant attention, she was sure — whoever he was dealing with. The doctor examined her ankle and pronounced it sprained. 'Stay off it for a few days, say three or four, and then you should be as right as rain. The head wound will heal better if left uncovered.'

Alice felt like observing that she had no wish to be as right as rain. She wanted to feel depressed; fed up. Why, she couldn't have said. Maybe she didn't want Dominic to think she was happy with the way events had gone? That she was grateful — Heaven forbid — for the manner in which he'd

rescued her, taken care of her —
because he had; even she had to
acknowledge that.

The initial sight of the bedroom that
he carried her to once the doctor had
left, however, was more than sufficient
to raise her spirits — completely against
her will, of course. Luxurious didn't
seem an adequate adjective. Sumptuous
was more apt, she decided.

Dominic set her down upon a
heavily carved, damask-draped, four-
poster bed. It stood, impressively,
upon a raised platform and was flanked
by a pair of floor-to-ceiling windows.
Oak wardrobes filled an entire second
wall, while on a third was an open
fireplace. Before this was grouped a
chaise-longue and two winged armchairs. A low table held a bowl of
freshly picked, scented roses, several
glossy magazines, a carafe of water and
a glass, as well as a small bowl of very
expensive-looking chocolates. Had he
been expecting her? Or was the room
always kept in this state of readiness for

a guest? No, the more logical explanation must be that the housekeeper had prepared it while she was downstairs with the doctor.

At the foot of the bed was a chest holding a television and a DVD player, as well as a radio and CD player, all operable from a control panel by the side of the bed.

'The bathroom is through that door.' He indicated a doorway that she hadn't noticed before. 'I'll get Mrs Hopkins to bring you a walking stick, unless you want me to help you in there?' A wry smile quirked the corners of his mouth as he all too accurately interpreted her expression. The thought of Dominic helping her to the toilet was a horrifying one. 'No? I'll go and fetch Mrs Hopkins then — or Emily, as she prefers to be called.'

Once he'd gone, Alice eyed the phone that also sat by the bed. She'd need some clean clothes and underwear. She'd call Zoe. She had a key to Alice's flat. She could collect a few items and bring them to her here. Knowing her friend, she'd love a nose around this place, and she'd hadn't seen Zoe for a while now.

Before Alice could lift the receiver, however, there was a gentle knock on the bedroom door. It must be the housekeeper, Emily.

It was. The plump little woman Alice remembered from her interview with Dominic bustled into the room, a warm smile on her face, and a tray of what looked like coffee in her hands. Over her arm was hooked a walking stick.

* * *

A half hour passed while Alice enjoyed her coffee and made the most of her comfortable surroundings, a welcome novelty after the discomforts of tree dwelling. She then decided to try and limp her way into the bathroom. Emily had offered to help her, but Alice insisted she could manage alone.

The bathroom was every bit as

opulent as the bedroom. Done out in bronze marble, black and gold, it shrieked wealth at her. Dominic Falconer was clearly every bit as rich as rumour had painted him.

Next, she telephoned Zoe. 'I've had a bit of an accident,' she told her.

'I knew it!' Zoe cried. 'You fell out of that tree, didn't you? What have you broken?'

'Nothing. I've sprained my ankle. It's okay, I've seen a doctor.'

'Do you want me to drive over and fetch you? And I hope after this, you'll abandon — '

'Zoe! I've simply sprained an ankle, not broken my neck.'

'I know, but you can't stay up a tree. How will you climb up and down?'

'Um . . . I'm not actually up the tree.' Here came the tricky bit. Explaining where she was. Goodness knew what Zoe would think.

'Where are you then? In hospital?'

'I'm at the Manor.'

'The Manor? The Manor Hospital?

I've never heard of that.'

'No. Chelmleigh Manor.'

The silence lasted for several seconds. As Alice knew that it took a lot to silence Zoe, she deduced that her friend was truly shocked. Was this how the rest of the town would react when they knew she'd accepted shelter from Dominic Falconer? 'You know — Dominic Falconer's house.'

'Yes, I do know that, Alice. What I don't know is how on earth you ended up there — in enemy territory, so to speak.'

'He insisted. In fact, he virtually kidnapped me — '

'What?' Zoe shrieked. '*Kidnapped* you?'

'Well, maybe that's too strong a word,' Alice said hastily. She didn't want Zoe calling the police.

'Alice, for heaven's sake, explain.'

'It was his fault that I fell, so he felt duty-bound to look after me.' Her words limped to a halt. 'He just picked me up and brought me here — '

'Hang on. What do you mean, it was his fault you fell? Did he push you or something?'

'No. He wanted me to leave the wood, voluntarily, before he had us forcibly evicted, and — and I refused. So he threatened to come up and get me. I started to climb further up the tree, lost my grip and fell.'

'Oh, Alice!' Zoe gasped in horror.

'H-he caught me but I landed awkwardly, hence my sprained ankle.'

'So how is it his fault if he caught you? Sounds like he saved you from more serious injury.'

'Well, I wouldn't have been climbing at all but for him coming after me.'

'Oh, I see — I think.'

'Anyway, he brought me back here and called his doctor.'

'So-o,' Zoe mused, 'not quite the heartless pig you thought.' She was grinning now, Alice could tell. 'So, come on then, tell me all. What's he like when he's at home?'

'I don't know, I've barely seen him so

far. The reason I rang you is to ask you to bring me some clean clothes from the flat, but now you've mentioned collecting me, you could take me back home. He's refusing — the arrogant so-and-so,' she muttered.

'No way,' Zoe blurted in her customary blunt fashion. 'If he's to blame, he can look after you. But I will bring you some clothes. And here's a piece of advice. Forget the demo — '

'You know I can't do that.'

'Oh, for goodness sake. Okay. Give me an hour and I'll be there.'

Zoe was true to her word and within an hour was being ushered into Alice's bedroom. She had a bagful of clothes.

'Wow!' she breathed, once Emily had left them. 'You've certainly landed on your feet, my girl.'

'Unfortunate choice of wording,' Alice said drily. 'Seeing as how I can't actually put one foot to the ground.'

'Mmm, of course. Sorry.'

'I've been expecting to see you at the camp.' Alice had been hurt that her friend hadn't visited her.

Zoe looked uncomfortable. 'Richard asked me not to, especially in the light of the recent burglaries. It wouldn't look good.'

'What wouldn't? Coming to see your closest friend? I had nothing to do with the burglaries.'

'Don't be like that, Alice. It's difficult for Richard, given that he's still hoping to get some of the work on the leisure centre. And maybe you should stay away too, if you don't want to be cast in the same mould.'

It was more or less what Dominic had said to her.

★　★　★

After 24 hours, Alice was heartily sick of the bedroom — luxurious or not. She needed a change of scene. She decided to try and get down the stairs. She had a stick; it should be manageable if she took it slowly.

However, her optimism proved sadly

misplaced. She was barely halfway down when her ankle turned and mind-numbing pain shot up her leg. She moaned and clung to the banister for support, just as her head began to spin and her ears to ring. Oh no. She was going to faint . . .

'What the hell are you doing?' It was Dominic.

'I — I — ' But it was no good. No matter how she tried to hold it at bay, she was beginning to lose consciousness. She felt herself sway forward and saw Dominic leap the stairs three at a time. The next thing she knew, she was in his arms, blinking dazedly up at him.

'Oh, I'm — I'm so sorry,' she said haltingly, but quite genuinely. The very last place she wanted to find herself was in his arms.

'You do seem to be making it a habit to fall on me,' he retorted, but when she ventured a swift glance up at him she saw that in fact, he was grinning down at her, his eyes glinting with good humour. And to her amazement, Alice felt herself smiling back.

Their gazes clung, his darkening as it lowered to her mouth. It was as if he'd touched her there, so intense was that look. Alice felt her heart skip a beat and her pulse accelerate madly. What was happening to her? She couldn't be attracted to him; she simply couldn't be. He was her sworn enemy, the man she'd vowed to fight to the bitter end.

'If you're so insistent on coming downstairs, allow me to assist you,' he went on, for all the world as if what had just passed between them hadn't happened. 'In fact, I was wondering, would you join me for dinner?'

Alice, bemused, heard herself agreeing. 'But won't Belinda mind?'

'She won't be there. She's off to some party or other. It will just be you and I.' His eyes darkened once more as his gaze held hers.

He helped her down to the sitting room and led her solicitously to the settee; gently lifting her foot to rest on a low stool that was already positioned for her. Had he anticipated her agreement to dine with him? It seemed likely. He was always so sure of himself. She wondered whether any woman had ever turned him down? Or was she, Alice, the first one to give him a hard time?

'A glass of wine?' he asked once she was settled. 'I've got a very good Pinot Grigot open.'

'Um — thank you. Yes.'

The door opened and Emily put her head around it. 'Dinner will be ready in half an hour.' She, too, looked unsurprised to see Alice sitting there.

Alice felt a surge of vexation. Was she that predictable? For a second, she was sorely tempted to say she wanted to return to her room, but something stopped her.

In half an hour precisely, Dominic once again helped her into the dining room. This was every bit as expensively and tastefully furnished as the rest of the house — or what she'd seen of the rest of the house. Emily had prepared what could only be described as a feast. Cornets of smoked salmon were crammed full of prawns. A fillet of tender beef, wrapped in a pastry case and served with a rich red wine sauce, came next and to finish there were perfectly cooked crepes Suzette.

Throughout it all, to Alice's surprise, she and Dominic talked practically non-stop. He proved to be an intriguing combination of humorist and intellectual, and Alice found herself face to face with a man that she could very easily grow to like and admire.

Eventually, of course, they progressed from music and literature to the personal. 'Have you any family?' he asked her.

'None. Both my parents were killed six years ago in a motorway pile-up. I have no siblings.'

Dominic's expression conveyed his deep sympathy. 'It couldn't have been easy to be left alone like that at — what? Twenty-one? Two?'

'Twenty-two. Old enough to be able

to look after myself. What about you?'
She decided to change the subject. She
didn't like talking about herself. 'Do
you have any family?'

'I had a brother — married to
Belinda, as you know — but he died a
year ago of a heart attack. The same
thing happened to my father, and my
mother passed away not long after he
did. I always believed she died from a
broken heart.' His voice faded and his
eyes grew distant. 'That was almost six
years ago, too.'

'So, Belinda — ?'

'She's staying here for a while, just
while her house is sold and she finds
another. It shouldn't be for long.'

'I see. So you'll be living here alone,
eventually, then?'

'For a while, yes.'

Alice wondered if that meant he had
plans to marry? She hadn't heard
anything about a fiancée, but that's
what his words seemed to suggest. For
some completely unaccountable reason,
the notion depressed her.

'So,' he went on, 'do you have other relations? Aunts, uncles, cousins?'

'No, nobody. Both my parents were only children. I think that was why they only had me.' It had been a constant source of grief to her, the fact that she had no brother or sister. Suddenly her eyes stung with tears. Angry with herself for her show of weakness, she dashed them away. It must be her current state; she didn't usually tend to weep when speaking about her lonely situation.

Dominic was on his feet immediately. 'Alice, I'm so sorry. I've made you cry, talking about it.'

'No, really. I'm just being silly.' But despite her assertion, the tears quickened until she really was crying. Sobbing, in fact. Something she hadn't done in a very long time. Not since the moment, right after her parents had died, when she'd realised exactly how alone she was.

But Dominic ignored her protest. He strode to her, pulled her to her feet and straight into his arms.

10

Dominic's breath was sweet, the scent of the wine he'd drunk gently feathering her face. 'Alice,' he murmured throatily. 'Let me . . . ' But the power of speech seemed to desert him as his voice thickened and fragmented.

Instead, he gathered her closer, his eyes holding hers, and slowly, very slowly, lowered his mouth to hers.

Alice couldn't quite believe what was happening. What was he doing? Minute electric shocks began to spark all over her body as, in the next second, his mouth possessed hers, hungrily, passionately, incredibly. She was helpless against the force of her own longing, and suddenly she was kissing him back, her lips parting beneath his, her arms closing around him. It was as if she had been waiting for this one moment for all of her life. She forgot everything else but the feel of him, his mouth upon hers, his body against hers.

Then, 'No! Stop — ' She dragged herself from his arms. 'What are you doing?' She staggered as she took an agonising step backwards, her injured foot giving way beneath her. Dominic's arm shot out and his hand gripped her arm, holding her steady, upright.

'Do I really have to tell you?'

'You were — were — ' Now it was she that was rendered speechless.

'Kissing you,' he said flatly, 'yes. What's wrong with that? We're both adults. We know what we're doing — '

'Do we? I'm not sure I do.' Her voice shook, the tears once more starting to her eyes. It was all too much in her weakened state. 'It shouldn't have happened. It *can't* happen.' She shook his hand off her.

'Alice . . . ' he began, his look softening, seeing the depth of her distress.

'No.' Cautiously she took another step back, putting a safe distance between them. 'I want to go home. I *need* to go home.' Her voice wobbled again. 'I can't stay here — not now.'

'You can't go,' he bluntly told her. 'It's ten-thirty at night. We've both had wine. I can't drive now.'

'Doesn't matter,' she mumbled. 'I'll call a taxi.'

Alice was appalled at what she'd just allowed to happen. She'd let Dominic Falconer, the man she was supposed to be fighting, to kiss her. What had she been thinking of? What had *he* been thinking of?

Wait a minute. Did he think that by making love to her, he'd win her round to his viewpoint, and that she'd stand aside while he did his worst? Was he really that cold-blooded? She stared at him, horrified at the very idea. It was absolutely imperative that she get away — now, while she could.

Dominic had been watching her expressive face closely and she saw his face harden. Could he have read her thoughts?

'I'll call the cab for you.' His voice was harsh, cruel. 'We can't have you staying here against your will, can we?'

Why not? was Alice's silent response to that. *After all, I've been kept here against my will right from the start.*

But ten minutes later, just as she'd demanded, Alice was sitting in the back of a taxi, on her way home.

Meanwhile, in a house nearby, a man surreptitiously forced a window and climbed in. He made his silent way to a bureau, opened it and inside found a cash tin. He grinned and removed all of the money therein. He slid the notes into his pocket and grinned even more broadly. So easy. He was on his way back to the window again when a voice spoke from the doorway.

'Right. I'm going to have you this time!'

The thief ran to the window and dived through it, head first, landing heavily on one shoulder and knee. He managed to get up and run across the garden to scale the fence. Then, despite his injuries, he ran for his life.

The man watching him get away noted the eagle emblazoned on the back of his jacket.

Alice, in the back of the taxi, saw the man running — well, limping, really, along the pavement. She too saw the jacket. Star! He was hurt.

'Stop,' she cried to the taxi driver. Please stop.'

The taxi screeched to a halt. The running man heard it and glanced over his shoulder. Alice gasped. It wasn't Star. It was someone wearing a jacket exactly like Star's. Someone she knew.

★ ★ ★

Alice hobbled into her flat. What should she do? Ring the police? Tell them what she suspected? That it hadn't been Star breaking into the houses; it had been someone wearing an exact copy of Star's jacket? Her sense of what was right was telling her to. To clear Star. But that would mean shopping someone else that she knew very well. She agonised for several long minutes, but her conscience insisted there was only one thing she could do — no matter who was hurt in the process.

She rang the police. 'Has a burglary been reported in the last few minutes?'

'Yes,' the police officer answered. 'In Poplar Road.'

Two minutes from where Alice had seen the man running.

'I think I've just seen the man who did it. He was running, and he was wearing a jacket with an eagle on the back. And I know it wasn't Star, the protester — I saw his face.'

'Right,' the policeman said. 'Where was he? I'll get a squad car out.'

'Wait! I know who he is. He'll probably go straight home. He didn't see me, so he won't know that I know him.'

'So who was it?'

'Sam Willis,' Alice shakily told him.

'He's clearly been impersonating Star, the protester, in an attempt to discredit all of them. His brother, Richard, is hoping to get the building work for the new centre. I suspect that he's hoping that by inciting local residents to fight back against the protesters, they'll succeed in driving them away so that work can begin. We've already had one incidence of that, with people throwing stones and all sorts. I was hurt in the process . . . '

Once she'd replaced the phone — the policeman had promised to go straight round and question Sam — it occurred to Alice to wonder how Zoe was going to take the fact that her best friend had been the one to shop her brother-in-law to the police. But what was worrying Alice even more — providing the burglar really had been Sam, of course — was the question of whether Richard was involved in his younger brother's actions. She'd go and see Zoe first thing tomorrow and try and explain her actions.

* ★ ★

Despite her reluctance, the first thing Alice did the next morning was to go and see Zoe. She'd rung the police station first and been told that Sam Willis had indeed been arrested. He'd been found in possession of the incriminating jacket and a substantial amount of money. The exact amount that had been stolen from the house in Poplar Road.

'And — and his brother, Richard?' Alice nervously asked.

'Mr Richard Willis knew nothing about it,' the policeman told her. Alice breathed a sigh of relief. If Richard had been carted off to the police station too, Zoe would never have forgiven her.

As it was, Zoe was upset and confused. She kept asking, 'Whatever possessed Sam?'

Alice had to know for sure. After all, Sam might have refused to incriminate his brother and so lied about Richard's involvement, 'Zoe, Richard didn't know what Sam was doing, did he?'

Zoe glared at her friend. 'Of course he didn't. He's as shocked as I am. What do you think he is? Sam was simply trying to help Richard — to secure the contract for the building work. He thought, apparently, that the local people would be so incensed at one of the protesters stealing from them, that they'd drive them away. So he stitched a cut-out eagle onto a denim jacket and then made sure he was seen running away from whichever house he'd broken into, so that he could then ring the police and say it was Star. It's a wonder he wasn't caught before.'

It was all just as Alice had supposed. It didn't make her feel any better, though, to know she'd been right.

'Stupid, stupid boy!' Zoe cried out.

Alice felt dreadfully guilty. Maybe she shouldn't have called the police? But she couldn't let an innocent man take the blame.

She eventually left Zoe and went

straight to the camp. Her first job was to find Crusoe. Eden was with him, and her glance spoke volumes. *Keep away from Crusoe.* Alice had every intention of doing just that. After her kiss with Dominic, she realised that anything she had felt for Crusoe was just a shadow of real emotion.

Crusoe, however, was oblivious to the undercurrents running between the two women. 'Hi, Alice,' he greeted her smilingly. 'How's the ankle? You're still limping, I see. Should you be here?'

'I'm not staying,' she told him. She pretended she hadn't seen the look of relief that crossed Eden's face. 'I don't think I'd be able to climb my tree any more. However, where's Star?' She looked around for the young man. 'I've got some news for him — well, for you all, really.'

'He's gone into town,' Crusoe said. 'Tell me and I'll be sure to pass on the message when he gets back.'

So Alice told them about the arrest of Sam for the burglaries.

'Wow! So Star's in the clear.' Even Eden's face brightened at the news.

'Yes.' Alice looked around then. The camp site still looked exactly the same as when she'd left it. 'No signs of the men with chainsaws yet? No-one's been to try and evict you?'

'No, nothing's been happening at all. Did Falconer mention anything to you about it?'

'No. I've barely seen him.' She averted her gaze from Crusoe's open one. She hated lying, but she wasn't about to confess that she and Dominic had shared a few moments of unforgettable passion.

'Okay. Well, keep in touch.'

'I will,' she promised. 'I might even be back at some point. Depends what happens, really.' In all honesty, however, she doubted she'd be returning. She needed to get back to her job. Neil had been very patient, but she fully expected a request to return to work any day now. Especially as she hadn't managed to submit more than a couple of pages of her diary.

It was strange, now she came to think of it, that Dominic hadn't raised the subject of the protest and his threatened eviction. He'd had her at his mercy, after all. But he hadn't made any attempt to persuade her to see reason, or to use her influence with the protesters to ask them to leave. For the first time since she'd left Chelmleigh Manor, she wondered why.

Could it have been him behind Sam's treachery, rather than Richard? But surely Sam would have told the police that? Wouldn't he? Unless, of course, Dominic had made it worth his while to stay silent?

★   ★   ★

She returned to a warm welcome from Neil. 'Glad to have you back,' he told her. She realised, looking at him, that she felt nothing for him any more. He was just a good friend, that was all. Was that down to the power of Dominic's kiss too, and the emotions it had unleashed? What a mess she was in. She couldn't deny her feelings any longer. She was in love with Dominic Falconer, and had been for some time, she realised. How on earth had that happened?

Hopefully, it would just be a fleeting thing. Over as swiftly as it had come. Perhaps, if she didn't see him again . . .

But that wasn't to be.

That evening, just as she was sitting down to eat her supper, there was a knock on her door. Was it Zoe, come to smooth things over between them? They'd parted on slightly acrimonious terms, Zoe understandably blaming her, in part, for Sam's arrest.

Alice went swiftly to the door. She flung it open, saying, 'Zoe, I'm so pleased — Oh.' She did a double-take. 'It's you.'

It was Dominic, and, for the first time in all of their acquaintance, he looked nervous and unsure of himself.

'Oh well, it's good to see you again

too,' he returned, the expression of uncertainty instantly replaced with one of sardonic amusement. 'You're obviously fully recovered — well, your tongue is, at any rate.'

'Sorry. You took me by surprise. I was expecting someone else.'

'Someone called Zoe, obviously. A friend?' His eyebrow lifted in the fashion to which she'd become so accustomed. This time, instead of inspiring irritation, it induced a rapid beating of her heart.

'Yes. She's my best friend, actually. It was her brother-in-law who's been arrested — '

'Yes, I heard about it.'

Alice eyed him suspiciously. He looked very unsurprised at the news. Was it indeed him who had put Sam up to it?

He sighed with exasperation. 'Oh, no. Don't say I'm going to be accused of instigating that too, along with all my other sins, imagined or otherwise? I can assure you, it had absolutely nothing to do with me. Whatever mistakes I might have made in my life, inducing a young man to commit burglary isn't one of them. I have always endeavoured to stay on the right side of the law, whether I agree with it or not. I haven't even indulged in bribery or corruption, despite what you clearly thought.'

To Alice's astonishment and considerable relief, she believed him.

He tilted his head to one side, regarding her almost bemusedly. 'Well, are you going to ask me in or do I have to say what I've come to say here on the doorstep?'

'Oh! Um, sorry, no — do come in.' She hoped only she could detect the tremor in her voice. What on earth could he want? Once they were inside and the door was closed behind them, the only thing she could say was a blurted, 'So what do you want?'

The gold flecks appeared in his eyes. Absently, she wondered what they indicated. Anger? Amusement?

She'd never known — despite the number of times she'd seen them now.

'You,' was his equally blurted response.

Alice shrugged. 'Okay. Well, here I am. Say what you've come to say.'

A strange expression crossed his face at that. Could it be uncertainty again? Surely not.

'Okay. I'm in love with you.' His voice shook ever so slightly.

Alice stared at him, mouth dropping open. 'Wh-what?'

A smile lifted his mouth. 'I'm in love with you — with every fibre of my being — and have been almost from the first second that I saw you.'

'B-but you can't be!' she stuttered. 'You've done nothing but berate me since — since — '

'Yes, well, you do have a knack of getting under my skin — as well as into my arms. Not always in the most sensitive or endearing way.'

'Well, it wasn't intentional,' she said stiffly, 'I can assure you of that. It just seemed to happen that way. And after all, you were — are — intending to destroy something very precious to me.'

'We'll talk about that aspect of things later.' His glance smouldered at her from beneath lowered eyelids, raking her from head to foot.

Alice felt distinctly uncomfortable. Was that what he intended? She wasn't dressed to receive guests. She had on a baggy T-shirt, old jeans and a pair of thick woollen socks. Her hair was unbrushed and her face bare of make-up. How could he possibly want her? Was this yet another ploy to undermine her?

'How's the ankle?' he unexpectedly asked. 'I see you've no shoes on. Still hurting, is it?'

'A bit, but it's healing up well.'

'Good. Well, now that that's the polite preliminaries dispensed with, can we get back to my reason for being here?'

'I'm still not sure exactly what that is,' she said. She didn't trust his declaration of love. He had to be playing some sort of game. After all, they were sworn enemies.

'To talk about us,' he told her.

'I'm not sure there is any 'us'.'

'Oh, I think there is.' His gaze narrowed even further. 'The wonderful woman I kissed was definitely not indifferent to me.'

'Well,' Alice began defensively, 'you took me by surprise, that's all. It was an instinctive reaction. If I'd known what was coming — '

'Oh, really. *If you'd known*. I see.' He tilted his head sideways again, and considered her reflectively. 'In that case, we'll try it again, shall we?'

Alice stared, horrified. 'T-try it again?'

'Yes. See what sort of response we get now — now that you've been warned, so to speak?'

'No, I don't think so.' Her eyes flicked from side to side, seeking escape.

'Are you frightened?'

Terrified, she could have said truthfully, but didn't. 'No, of course not. Why should I be frightened?' She tried a snort of contempt, but all she emitted was a squeak of terror.

'Well, let's see, shall we?' And he reached for her.

Alice, desperate to avoid any sort of physical contact between them — for how could she possibly hide her love for him if he should start kissing her? — took a hasty and ill-considered step back. The inevitable happened. Her injured foot gave way beneath her and she stumbled.

Dominic instantly made a grab for her and caught her before she could fall back. 'Here we go, falling into my arms yet again,' he murmured huskily. 'Not that I'm complaining.'

'Hadn't you noticed?' she retorted. 'I wasn't falling into your arms but away from them.'

She tried to push him away, but he simply took hold of her hands and pushed them down behind her. He then

185

pulled her in close to him, and gazed deep into her nervous eyes, before groaning, 'Oh, Alice, if only you knew . . . ' and then proceeding to kiss her with an expert and much practised thoroughness.

Alice fought for a very brief second before her emotions took over and she melted against him, passion and desire racing through her, conquering any sort of resistance she might be tempted to offer.

The kiss went on and on, until Dominic finally released her two hands. She slid them up his chest and around his shoulders, to entwine at the back of his neck. All the while, his lips ravished hers, and his arms held her so tightly, she could feel every hard line of him. She adored him. Why go on fighting this feeling?

Hours later, it seemed, they pulled apart, Dominic breathing heavily, Alice flushed and tingling.

'Well!' He smiled down into her misty eyes. 'I think that settles the matter. Just say it — please. I want to hear you say it.'

She capitulated, totally and willingly. 'Yes, I love you. I can't help it. I know I shouldn't — '

But before she could finish whatever it was she was about to say, he'd captured her mouth again. She stood quite still, letting him make love to her for a while longer, but she knew — as did he — that there were things they had to discuss.

She pulled away from him, disregarding his groan of disappointment.

'I know, I know,' he said. 'We have to talk — '

'Yes. I have to know what's going to happen to the wood. I can't be with the man who's about to destroy it — no matter how much I love him.'

'It's all sorted. I'm moving it.'

'Moving it?' Alice gasped. 'The wood? How on earth — ?'

'No, not the wood.' He grinned delightedly. 'The wood is quite safe.

There's a much better site, a couple of miles away. I don't know why I didn't consider that in the first place. Just some empty fields; no trees, no dear little red squirrels. Nothing to upset the woman I'm madly in love with. I've already applied for planning consent for that site. Shouldn't be any problem, I've been told.'

'Really?' She gazed at him, wide-eyed.

'Yes, really.' He tenderly mimicked her breathless response.

'Oh, Dominic.'

'So now that that's all cleared up, I have another question for you.'

'Yes?' There was an intriguing look in his eyes. Alice held her breath. What was coming now?

Tenderly he took her hand and asked, 'Will you marry me?'

'*M-marry* you?' Whatever she'd expected, it hadn't been that. She'd hoped for it, of course, eventually, but — It was too much. Her heart sang.

Dominic waited, a flicker of nervousness making itself apparent. She loved him even more for that, for letting her see his vulnerability.

She couldn't keep him waiting any longer. 'Oh yes, my darling; yes, yes!' she sang. 'Yes.'

'Good,' he returned, all sign of nerves gone. 'So how does next month sound? Because I think I've waited quite long enough for you.'

Alice didn't reply. She couldn't. She was enfolded in his arms once more, her words smothered with the force of his kiss.

THE END

A TIME FOR DREAMS

Dawn Bridge

Claire is a teacher awaiting an Ofsted inspection at her school. She discovers that the chief inspector is her former fiancé, Adam whom she has not seen for five years. Although Claire is now in a relationship with Martin, she is overcome with guilt when she realises she still has feelings for Adam. Suddenly she has to confront her past and decisions have to be made.

THE HEART SHALL CHOOSE

Wendy Kremer

Roark is charming, but emotionally damaged by his broken marriage. Julia quit a relationship when she found her ex-boyfriend was exploiting her. Whilst Julia still hopes to find real love one day, Roark intends to shut love out of his life altogether. Working in a tour company together, their friendship grows - but can Julia storm the barriers that surround his heart? And can Roark forget the past and move on to a better future, before it's too late?

THE JUBILEE LETTER

Carol MacLean

The letter had been lost in the post for fifty years. But for Avril it solved a mystery, which had unsettled her since the Queen's Coronation — when she was young and in love . . . There had been two suitors to choose from: was Avril tempted by charming Jack or quiet Gordon? Both Jack and Gordon had secrets, and it was only when Avril discovered what they were hiding that she had been able to choose a love to last a lifetime.

RISING TIDE

Roberta Grieve

Separated from her childhood sweet-heart Adam, due to a family feud, Grace Brownlow agrees to marry the man chosen for her by her parents. But there are secrets in Thomas's past, as she discovers when she accompanies him back to India. Meanwhile, on his way to India, Adam is hoping to see Grace once more and reassure himself that she is well and happy. But Grace is in trouble. Will Adam arrive in time to help her?